PRAIRIE NIGHTS

PRIMROSE SERIES
BOOK TWO

TANYA RENEE

For all of those that have lost faith in love. Your happily ever after is out there. Just believe.

ALSO BY TANYA RENEE

Primrose Series

Prairie Sky

Prairie Nights

Prairie Fire

PROLOGUE

*W*hitney Faris peeled her eyes open, mascara caked to her eyelashes. Immediately assaulted by a harsh stream of light escaping the thick hotel room curtains, she squinted as she tried to figure out where she was.

A wall of warmth to her back and a soft snore made her eyes widen as memories of the night before came at her in a flashback. Very dirty memories of the man next to her. Alcohol infused memories rolling through her mind like a theatre reel. *Oh my God.*

She sat up quietly, taking a moment to regain her equilibrium, her head spinning from the intoxication of last night. Glancing down at herself, the thin hotel room sheet barely covering her naked breasts, she winced as her eyes darted to her left to the very naked, very sexy, Hayden Hastings. Facing away from her, she unapologetically let her eyes roam over his muscular back and taut behind not covered by the sheet. *Damn, he's sexy. Damn, he knew exactly what to do with that magnificent body.* Her eyes widened in panic. *Damn, this is not something I do.* A wave of regret washed over her. *What have I done?*

At 34, Whitney wasn't the kind of woman that went home with men she barely knew. She wasn't the kind of woman who went home with anyone. This was not her modus operandi, ever. Seven years out of an emotionally abusive marriage, she had dated a lot, but had never gone home with a man. Especially a man she had known less than 24 hours. *What was I thinking?*

Groaning internally at the awkward situation she found herself in, Whitney slipped out of the bed as silently as she could, trying not to disturb the hot as hell man fast asleep in the hotel room bed. Naked, she searched for her clothing, finding her bra and panties in the corner and her green cocktail dress lying in a crumpled pile next to a chair. Flashes of their frantic undressing clouding her thoughts as she considered how he expertly removed her dress and underwear as he kissed, sucked, and bit at her skin. *Oh God, he knew just how to use his tongue.* Her core pulsated at the vision of his head buried between her legs. That was before...her thoughts trailed off as all that they had done last night came back to her in a rush. The soreness between her thighs, a stark reminder.

I need to get out of here, panic taking over. *Before he wakes up and I'm subjected to an awkward morning after conversation.* Quickly putting on her bra and panties, she slipped back into her wrinkled dress, thanking all the yoga classes for the flexibility she had so she could zip herself up.

Taking a quick look at her reflection in the full-length

hotel room mirror, she shook her head at her disheveled reflection. *This is not you. This is not who you are.* Quickly smoothing down her shoulder-length blonde hair and finger combing through the tangles, she wiped away the black flakes of mascara from under her deep brown eyes.

Hayden stirred, murmuring in his sleep. She stilled, waiting to see if he would wake and praying to the gods that he wouldn't. His steady snore returned, causing her to sigh with relief as she slipped her clutch under her arm and grabbed her high heels. Tiptoeing towards the hotel room door, she stole one last glance at the gorgeous man fast asleep in the rumpled bed and exited the room, for her very first walk of shame.

*H*ayden Hastings nursed his beer as he sat at the head table watching wedding guests dance and groove to a compilation of popular 80s tunes. The whir of the heaters making the large white tent warm and inviting as well as adding their slow hum to the already loud music, laughter, and chatter of the guests. Where he sat, he had a perfect view of the most beautiful woman he had ever laid eyes on: Whitney Faris. She moved to the music; her petite figure willowy but curvaceous in all the right places. Memories of their one night together three weeks prior, when he touched, tasted, and devoured every inch of that gorgeous body rolled through his mind on repeat. How incredibly soft her skin was under his touch. How she tasted on his tongue. The delectable sounds she made as he pleasured her. Each naughty memory making his heart pound faster and arousal burned low in his belly.

Whitney Faris was not like any other woman he had met before. On top of being drop dead gorgeous, she was an incredibly sophisticated city girl who carried herself with an air of grace and confidence he had never encountered before. Sharp and witty, with a laugh that was heartfelt and contagious. In his eyes, Whitney was the complete package.

After their mind-blowing, albeit intoxicated night together, resulting in her unexpectedly hasty exit, he was, as expected, not sure where she stood with him. Without question, he wanted to know more about her, but did she want to get to know him? From the sly glances she kept stealing his way, he had a gut feeling she did.

"Hey, brother. Why aren't you on the dance floor?"

Hayden looked up to his newly married big brother, Ben Hastings, his blue eyes questioning. "Just enjoying the view." He replied, tipping the neck of his beer towards Whitney, laughing and shaking her backside on the dance floor.

Ben's gaze followed his gesture, and he turned back to his brother with an acknowledging grin. "Are you interested in Whitney?" he asked, taking a seat next to Hayden. "She's a pretty great girl."

"Yeah, sexy as hell too." Hayden remarked, not peeling his eyes off her.

Ben frowned and gave his brother his signature scowl. Hayden glanced at Ben, catching his scrutinizing glare. "Put your critical thoughts away, Ben." he said, giving his brother the side eye. "I know you always have an opinion on my love life."

"I just think you need to take it easy, Hayden." Ben replied, giving him a knowing look. "You always jump in feet first and end up getting hurt in the process."

Hayden took a long sip of his beer and his eyes settling on his brother, knowing he was right. Hayden's dating "antics" had become the stuff of legend in Primrose. As a successful, handsome business owner, and eligible guy in his late 20s, he had become a hot commodity for all the single ladies in town and for all "the desperate to marry off their daughters mothers" trying to set him up. But behind all his ultimate single guy persona lay a self admitted hopeless romantic. He wanted more than anything to find his one person and was never afraid to put himself out there to make it happen. Even if it meant he fell flat on his face or, quite often in his case, had his heart broken.

"Do you think Whitney would hurt me?" he asked with a small chuckle, thinking his brother was absurd to think so.

"No, I'm more concerned that you're going to hurt her."

Hayden took in his brother's offhanded comment, his face morphing into a deep frown. "Why would you say that?" he asked, now thoroughly annoyed with his brother.

"I'm not saying you would intentionally hurt her, Hayden." Ben clarified. "But you need to be careful with her. I don't know her entire story. But I know she was married before, and it ended badly," he informed. "From what Ever has mentioned, she doesn't have the best track record when it comes to dating and she's very guarded with her heart." Hayden turned to Ben, his eyes full of questions and imploring him to continue. "All I know is she was married young, and he was not a nice guy, if you know what I mean," Ben continued, giving Hayden a wary look.

"Abusive?" Hayden asked, his brows furrowing.

"No idea. I don't think Ever even knows all the details. Just that it was a very bad situation, and she's been divorced for at least five years now."

Hayden slowly returned his gaze to the stunning woman confidently shaking her body on the dance floor. The information Ben just provided, not adding up to him. She carried herself with so much confidence. He would never have known that she had been through so much, let alone, have experienced a failed marriage.

"I'm just saying if you're going to pursue her, make sure you treat her well."

"I always treat the girls I date well!" Hayden replied, locking his brother with a defensive stare.

"What I mean, Hayden, is that Whitney is not a conquest. She's not that kind of woman," Ben explained, referring to his presumed history of promiscuity. "Just be careful with her."

Frustrated, Hayden turned away from his brother and brought his beer bottle to his mouth for a long pull. Although Ben's words stung, Hayden understood his track record looked bad as an outsider looking in. A string of short-term relationships, perceived as flings. Yet Hayden prided himself on treating each woman he dated like gold and had never dated more than one woman at a time, choosing to give each woman his entire focus. In fact, he would more accurately label himself as a serial monogamist. It was not his intention to ever hurt anyone, and, in the end, he was usually the one that got hurt. Of course, his brother, with his limited dating history, didn't see it that way and that both frustrated and disappointed him.

Tamping down his building agitation, his eyes drifted towards Whitney again, who was laughing with Bea and Ever, her beautiful face glowing. *Damn, she's gorgeous.*

If he were lucky enough to date a woman like Whitney Faris, he would prove to her and everyone else that he was worthy of a deep and meaningful relationship. He just needed to be given the chance.

* * *

WHITNEY COULDN'T KEEP her eyes off Hayden. His continuous bold glances and sexy smiles as he glanced over at her did not help. Nor did the memories of their one crazy drunken night together. The simple thought of that wild night made her flush red, and her pulse quicken. His eyes raked over her body over and over as she danced, making her desire build and her heart flutter rapidly in her chest. Avoiding eye contact, she surveyed the guests, willing herself to not glance his way again. As annoying as his persistent attention was, part of her liked it a lot.

Too many questions floated around in her head. *Does he want to come talk to me? What would we talk about? Would he ask me why I left so unceremoniously that morning? Would we talk about how his tongue teased my breasts as he drove into me? Dear Lord, Whitney, get your mind out of the gutter,* she chided herself as her traitorous eyes inadvertently stole yet another glance his way. This time their eyes met, evoking a sly smile from his lips and a warm flood of heat crept up her body and settled in her cheeks. Hayden was sex personified and far too handsome, so in her eyes that made him dangerous.

"Are you okay?" Ever asked Whitney, seeing her rosy face as she followed her stare towards Hayden.

"Yes, sorry, I'm fine…" she trailed off, pulling her gaze from him, the hue of her face deepening at being caught ogling Ever's new Brother-in-law.

Ever's eyes drifted between Hayden to Whitney and a knowing smirk tugged at her lips as she inquired, "Do you like Hayden?"

Whitney's eyes darted to her friend and her mouth opened to deny her observation, but Ever held up her hand, snuffing out her rebuttal. "You can deny it all you want, but the looks you have been giving each other all night and quite frankly, since Ben's proposal in Toronto, speak for themselves." She commented, putting her hands on her hips. "Did something happen between you two in Toronto?"

Whitney's eyes widened at her friend's question, feeling a bead of sweat form on her brow. *How was Ever always so perceptive?* Whitney hadn't told a soul about her one-night stand with Hayden. *Had Hayden told Ben? Did Ben mention it to Ever?* Her head started spinning and Whitney offered Ever a feigned look, hoping it would disguise the truth.

"Again, no need to say anything." Ever continued. "I can tell you two shared more than simply conversation, but I don't need the details," she said, putting her hands up in the air again as she added, "I will say this, Whitney. Hayden is a truly a good guy. Yes, he's a little flirty and has done his share of dating around, but I have gotten to know him well, and he is truly awesome. I personally think he just needs to find the right woman for him."

"So, he sleeps around?" Whitney inquired; eyebrows raised in question.

"I don't think so. Everyone seems to have labeled him as a playboy, but I don't think he is at all." she explained. "I know for a fact; he's looking for something more meaningful."

As Whitney was about to reply, a warm hand touched her shoulder, and she swung around, meeting Hayden's gorgeous blue eyes causing her to swoon. *Seriously, those eyes.* Whitney's breath stilled when he leaned down to whisper in her ear, his hot breath causing goosebumps to form on her skin as his cheek gently brushed hers.

"Did you want to dance?"

Ever smiled at them, her eyes sparkling with amusement as she said. "Have fun." And slowly walked away, searching for her new husband.

Whitney watched Ever go, her eyes flitting back to his and getting lost for a moment before she stuttered out her answer. "Ah, yes, sure. Why not!" she exclaimed, awkwardly trying to get her bearings. *Seriously Whitney.*

Hayden let out a deep chuckle and took her hand, leading her to the dance floor. Swinging her around in a flourish, making a shocked and delighted giggle escape her throat, he pulled her close, his hard, muscular body flush with hers.

Her heart fluttered wildly as they swayed to the Journey ballad drifting from the speakers. Nervousness coiled in Whitney's belly at their proximity, and his intoxicating cologne swirled around her, befuddling her thoughts. *Say something, say something.* "80's music is the best!" she blurted out, far louder than she intended. *Are you kidding me, Whitney?*

Hayden met her eyes, an amused smile slowly curling his lips as he replied, "It's pretty good. I was born in 1993, so it's not what I grew up listening to."

Whitney's eyes widened as she met his gaze, the math calculating quickly in her head. "So, you're 28?" she questioned, feeling her heart sink at the realization. *6 years younger than me.*

He nodded with his sexy smirk. "That's right, and you are what, 27 or 28?"

"I'm 34, Hayden." she replied, holding his gaze, and searching for signs of rejection. *Nothing.* Whitney swallowed down, her mouth drying as the realization that she slept with a much younger man slowly sunk in. Suddenly overwhelmed, she stepped out of his hold.

Hayden's eyes widened in surprise. "Is something wrong?" he asked, confusion covering his face as he reached out for her hand, only to have her move further away from him.

"I just need a moment," she replied, giving him a "just let me go" look, then turned and left the dance floor.

HAYDEN STOOD DUMBFOUNDED as Whitney left the dance floor and disappeared amongst the guests. *What just happened?* Confusion, wrapping around his thoughts like a vice. *Was it something I said? Something I did?* He needed to find her and talk to her about this. Searching the crowd, he caught sight of her slipping around the side of the house and followed.

As he rounded the farmhouse, he spotted her down the path leading to the paddocks at the back of the barn. The horses whinnied as she approached them. Halfway down the path, he stopped to watch her for a moment as she greeted the horses and leaned down to pick some of the long grass that edged the fence. She patted a horse's neck as it pulled the grass from her hand, and he could hear her faint giggle as she reached down to grab more for the insistent horses. Continuing down the path, she glanced behind her, hearing his footsteps.

"You're spoiling them," he commented as he reached her and leaned against the paddock fence. A horse now coming to greet him, he offered it a scratch and turned towards her adding. "You abandoned me on the dance floor back there."

Whitney stole a sideways glance at him, her eyes flitting away as she patted the horse nudging her for attention. "I'm sorry, Hayden. I needed a moment to think." She replied, embarrassment in her tone.

"Now that you've had a moment, please explain to me what that was all about?" he pushed, stepping a little closer to her. "Is it the age thing? Because I have no problem with you being older than me," he confessed, slowly bridging the gap between them.

Whitney let out a guffaw and turned to face him, defiantly raising her chin as their eyes met. "You say that now, Hayden, but I think my life experience may be a little too much for you."

"Try me," he replied, stepping even closer, his eyes boring into hers.

"I really don't know you well enough to explain," she replied, taking a step back as the sexual tension between them grew palpable.

Hayden cocked an eyebrow at her and flashed her his sexy smile.

Flustered, a rosy blush returned to her cheeks as she stuttered, "You know what I mean, Hayden." His smile deepened. *Surely, I'm going to hell for taunting her.* Letting out a frustrated growl, she exclaimed, "Stop looking at me that way!"

"In what way am I looking at you?" he asked, as he stepped closer, the intense heat permeating the mere inches that separated them.

"Like you want a repeat of Toronto." she replied, meeting his gaze, her feet firmly planted in place.

Desire at her words quelled inside him as he reached out to grip her by the waist and pulled her closer. Her breath caught and lashes fluttered as her resolve dissipated. They were so close, his mouth craving hers as their breaths mingled hot and heady.

"What are you doing?" she asked him huskily, her chest heaving with each breath.

Instead of answering, he persisted, "Tell me you don't want to kiss me again, Whitney."

Whitney gazed up hazily into his intense, lust filled eyes and what was left of her resolve vanished as their lips crashed together. He lifted her off the ground, her legs wrapping around his waist, the need to devour her overtaking him. A needy moan escaped her lips as they parted, inviting him to deepen their embrace. Tongues tangling, he backed her towards the barn, shielding them from view as he pressed her against the wall. Lips roaming down the column of her neck, he murmured against her ear, "See, I know what you want."

She shivered under his words, her chest heaving as he kissed a path down the side of her neck to trace her collarbone. Eyes closing in pleasure, her body instinctively pressing into him, seeking friction, as his hands kneaded her behind, under her dress. "Hayden, we need to…" she was drowned out, as his lips recaptured hers in a deep, sensual kiss.

The chemistry they shared was like a match igniting. If they didn't stop, they were going to burst into flames. But he couldn't stop, his body craving hers like an addict needing a fix as he kissed a path to her cleavage.

"Hayden, we need to stop." She whimpered, and he paused, raising his gaze to hers. "Anyone could come this way and see us."

"I don't mind." he grinned wickedly as he leaned in to kiss her again.

Her hand pressed into his chest, and she met his clouded with lust eyes as she repeated. "We need to stop."

Hayden let out a long-pained exhale, and he connected his forehead to hers, as they emerged from their kiss drunk haze.

"Whitney, I like you, I like you a lot," Hayden confessed, huskily. "I want to see you again."

"I like you too, Hayden." she replied, meeting his hopeful gaze.

"Then let me get to know you more," he offered,

setting her back down on her feet and helping her straighten out her dress.

"I think you know me pretty well already." She chortled, smoothing down her hair.

"But I want to really get to know you," he continued.

"Like friends?"

"Like friends with a sordid history," he replied, waggling his eyebrows.

Whitney cocked her head to the side and searched his eyes, checking the sincerity in his request. Despite their hot little make-out session against the barn wall, he wanted to be friends with her. He wanted to know what made her tick.

"So, are you asking me for my phone number?" she asked playfully.

"Yes, that would be a start."

She guffawed, and he understood how absurd the situation appeared. Two minutes ago, he was grinding his body into hers, his tongue exploring her mouth as he imagined himself sinking deep into her and now, he was asking for her phone number.

Whitney returned her gaze to his, an ironic mix of rebuttal and hilarity in her eyes as she conceded, "Yes, Hayden, you can have my phone number."

CHAPTER 2

After Ben and Ever's wedding, Whitney returned to Toronto, settling back into her life in the city. Having been a city girl her entire life, she was surprised how much she enjoyed the slow pace of Primrose. The place had its own brand of charm, and the people were kind and friendly, always curious to know more about her and her life. Such a contrast from the city where anonymity was the norm. Getting a glimpse into small town life made her want to return, especially to see her dear friend, Ever, again.

The moment she and Ever met, they became fast friends and now she considered her more like a sister than one of her clients. Seeing Ever's art career take off and having been a part of it since the beginning, had bonded them. Now with her friend and number one client, married, hopelessly in love and no longer close, she felt alone and on the cusp of a change herself. *But what would that change be?* Having worked for Rosenburg Agencies for the past eight years she enjoyed her job, but often found her mind wandering to other ways she could make a living using her passion for creativity and art. Perhaps she could go into business for herself.

Entering Rosenburg Agencies, Whitney greeted the receptionist with a smile as she strode down the hall, fielding more greetings from her colleagues. Entering her office, she took a seat behind her desk, pulling out her phone and swiped it open. Two unread messages. With a smile, she clicked on the first one seeing Hayden's text.

Hayden: "Hey there, gorgeous! I hope you have an awesome day! Mind if I send you a dirty picture?"

A picture of a cute pink piglet covered in mud popped up on her screen.

Whitney shook her head and laughed. It had been a week since she had returned home from the wedding and Hayden had taken to texting her. His daily flirtatious and corny texts had quickly become one of her favorite parts of her day.

Whitney: "Hayden, that's not the kind of dirty picture I want to see. Where's that cute ass?"

A picture of a donkey baring its teeth to the camera popped up on her phone.

Whitney: "Lol, you're too funny! I'm at work now, but can we chat later?"

Hayden: "Yes, of course. Glad I made you smile, gorgeous. Have a wonderful day!"

Whitney grinned at his message, setting down her phone and leaning back in her chair. Hayden was a charmer and knew exactly how his comments affected her. Every time she read back their conversations, they left her feeling light and although she had no doubt that he wanted the opportunity to reignite their chemistry, she would be lying if she didn't admit to liking his positive attention. After a 7-year marriage that nearly broke her, a lacklustre dating life full of crazy circumstances and disappointing let downs, it was flattering, and she couldn't help but soak in every word and compliment.

Leaving their conversation, she clicked on the second notification. As the message popped up on her screen, an instant uneasiness settled in the pit of her stomach as she read it.

"Dumb whore, you thought you could just walk away from us. I know where you're hiding, and I will find you."

Her eyes frantically darted around her office as if he would appear. Glancing back to her phone, she checked the caller ID. Unknown number. It was Paul; she was sure of it. It had been five years since the threats stopped and the judge issued her a restraining order along with finalizing her divorce. Knowing the restraining order had expired recently, something in her gut told her it was him. *Why is he texting me? How did he get my number?* A familiar sense of panic and anxiety washed over her as flashbacks of how he would belittle, call her terrible names, and tell her she was worthless floated into her consciousness. Telling her no one would or could love her, except him. His harsh words and emotional abuse breaking down her soul and bruising her heart. At times throughout their marriage, she wished he would just hit her. That way, at least she had physical proof of the scars he was branding.

For five excruciatingly long years, she endured his slurs and anger filled rage until she finally found the courage to leave him. Paul, of course, was sorry, apologizing profusely, and made every attempt to get her back. After each failed attempt, more name calling would ensue. And after two years of separation with him dragging his heels on their divorce, he started ambushing her at work, insisting on seeing her. Once he found out where she lived, he would show up at her townhome door with flowers and gifts, begging for her forgiveness. Whitney knew then and there that she needed a restraining order. Shortly after she got protection, the judge granted her a divorce, and she changed her phone number, moving to a different part of the city. She didn't hear from him again. Until now.

What am I going to do? She questioned, rubbing her temples, her head pounding. She had worked so hard over the past five years to erase her past. She attended regular therapy, started practicing meditation and yoga to deal with her anxiety and panic attacks, and had acquired an incredible group of friends who loved and supported her. Whitney was proud of how far she had come and grateful for the happy existence she made for herself.

Suddenly, an unexpected knock sounded at her door, making her jump out of her seat.

"Oh Whitney, sorry, I startled you." Her boss, Ned Rosenburg, said as he stood in her doorway. "Is everything okay?" he asked, brows furrowing.

"Sorry Ned, yes, everything's fine. How can I help you?"

Ned entered her office and took a seat across from her, steepling his hands in front of him. Ned Rosenburg was in his mid 60s with salt and pepper hair and kind blue eyes. He opted for designer sweaters, tailored shirts, and chinos rather than suits for the office and had a laid-back, easy-going personality which Whitney appreciated. He was fiercely passionate about art and helped her build her portfolio of clients while always making himself available for help or questions. She couldn't think of a better boss to have.

"As you know, I just turned 65 and my husband, David, just retired this past spring." He explained. "We recently celebrated my birthday in Costa Rica and fell in love with the culture there."

"Yes, I saw all your pictures on social media!" she exclaimed excitedly. "Costa Rica looks heavenly."

"It was," he replied, looking towards the window behind her as if reflecting. Returning his gaze to her, he continued. "David has convinced me to retire, and we're moving down there as of December 1st."

"Oh, wow! Seriously Ned, that's incredible!"

"Thank you." he smiled, excitement flashing in his blue eyes, then quickly morphing into a frown. "Let me just pull off the bandage, Whitney. I've decided to close the office as of November 15th."

Whitney's eyes widened, disbelief tightening her chest. "That's in three weeks."

Ned reached out, resting his hand on hers as he offered her a reassuring smile. "Whitney, you're an amazing agent and have built an enviable portfolio. I'll be splitting my portfolio up to distribute between you and several other agents here in the office. I have a handful of incredible artists out of Winnipeg, and I would like to pass those on to you."

"That is so sweet of you, Ned." she replied, still trying to grapple with the news.

Leaning back in his chair, Ned scrutinized her as he asked, "You're considering a change, am I right?" Whitney slowly blinked, unsure of how to answer. "I know you and Ever Wolton have become close friends and I know her moving away has been hard on you. I also know you have been through a lot in your life, Whitney." he continued with compassion in his eyes. "You forget you were new here when your marriage ended, and I saw what you went through with Paul, having to deal with his constant harassment. You deserve to be surrounded by those that support you. You should be close to your best friend."

"Change would be nice." Whitney agreed. "My parents are retired and moved to Arizona last year and my younger brother, Nick and his wife live on the East Coast, so really there isn't much holding me back from moving."

"I think now is the time to do it then. Just like David and I, sometimes you just need to follow the path that life leads you down," Ned said with a smile.

Whitney laughed, leaning back in her chair. "The path to Manitoba is likely a lot colder than Costa Rica, but yes, being closer to Ever would be amazing!"

"Good, it's settled. My Winnipeg clients are going to you!" he exclaimed, rising from his chair. "I'll understand if you want to leave the office early before we close the doors. Moving provinces is a big deal. You'll have to figure out your living arrangements."

"Thanks Ned! I appreciate it and I'll take you up on that," she replied as she rose from her desk and walked with him to the door.

With a final thank you, she returned to her desk, stopping in front of the large window overlooking the city below. Sighing, a sense of peace came over her at the knowledge that this chapter of her life was closing and a new one was opening. Whitney loved Toronto, the hustle of the downtown, the incredible skyline, the trails to walk along the lake and the beautiful parks all holding a piece of her heart. Undoubtedly, she would miss it. But now, with Paul resurfacing, this change was exactly what she needed.

HAYDEN ENTERED the storeroom of Hastings Hardware, passing the shelves of stock and headed towards his workshop at the back of the room. He made his way to his worktable and grabbed his leather tool belt, fastening it around his hips. Scanning the 2x4s against the wall, he picked one out and put it on the workshop table. As he reached for a set of clamps hanging on the wall, his phone rang, and he pulled it out of his back pocket, the name he was hoping to see flashing on the screen. *Whitney.* A grin tugged at his lips as he remembered their exchange earlier that morning and answered his phone. "Hey there, gorgeous, couldn't go another moment without talking to me?"

Her contagious laugh sounded at the end of the line, instantly warming his insides as she answered cheekily. "Don't flatter yourself, Hays."

"Hays! Already giving me pet names. You flatter me, Whit."

A huge guffaw sounded over the phone, and he could feel her beautiful brown eyes roll at his comment. Whitney was thoroughly adorable when she was flustered and annoyed with him, and he simply couldn't help himself.

"Is there a purpose to your call, other than flirting with me, of course?" he asked playfully as he leaned against his workbench and crossed his legs at the ankles.

"Ever and Ben are still on their honeymoon, correct?"

"Yes, for another ten days. Why do you ask?"

"Well, I was going to contact them, but maybe you could help me." She explained. "I just found out today that the agency I work for is closing down in three weeks and they passed on all their Winnipeg artists to me, so it looks like I'll be moving."

Hayden stood up straight, his ears perking up at the possibility of this amazing woman living closer to him. "Where are you planning to move, then?" he asked, sounding more eager than he intended.

"I was thinking of Primrose, or maybe St. Augustine. Honestly, I'm not sure right now. I was thinking of flying out next week to meet with a few clients and look at a few places. But I guess with Ben and Ever still away, I'll have to find a hotel to stay in."

"Come stay with me," he blurted, the words tumbling out before he gave them any thought. *Silence.* "I mean, I have plenty of room and honestly the house has been super quiet since Ben moved out." he continued trying to steady his words, knowing she may be apprehensive.

Silence filled the line until he heard Whitney let out a

long sigh. "Do you think that's a good idea?" she asked, her voice dripping with doubt.

"Because you can't keep your hands off me?" he asked teasingly. "Or because we have a history?"

"Yes." she cleared her throat, clarifying. "The history, not the hands." *How can I reassure her I want to help her?* Whitney continued, trying to explain herself. "Hayden, that crazy night we shared was not something I do. I don't sleep around, especially with a man I hardly know." She confessed, sounding sheepish.

Hayden ran his hands through his hair. He liked Whitney a lot. She was beautiful, smart, and so darn sexy it made his heart hurt. Knowing how uncomfortable she was talking about their one incredible night together and hearing the embarrassment in her voice, honestly frustrated him. Yes, their night together was unexpected, surprising them both. Yes, perhaps, they did take things a bit far considering their inebriated state, but for Hayden he wasn't sorry it happened. That night was the start of something that he desperately wanted to revisit. Despite his lingering desire for Whitney, he had Ben's words echoing in his ear–*Be careful with her.*

"I promise I'll be a complete gentleman." He reassured. "I respect how you feel about our history, and I would never knowingly do anything to make you feel uncomfortable." The continued silence was deafening. His brows furrowing in confusion as he asked, "Whitney, are you still there?"

"Yes." she replied, her voice sounding small.

"I'm offering this to you as a friend, and because I

know this is your best option." He added. "I would be happy to pick you up from the airport, too."

She let out another long sigh, replying. "Okay, Hays. That would be nice."

"Once you're here, we can figure out your living situation. Does that sound good?"

"Sounds perfect. Thank you so much, Hayden. You are very sweet to offer." She added, her voice sounding a little brighter.

"I try," he replied with all sincerity. "Send me your itinerary when you know when you're flying out."

* * *

WHITNEY HUNG UP HER PHONE, relief washing over her, followed by the sudden realization of what she just agreed to. Staying with Hayden, in his home, just the two of them. He was temptation on a stick. Whitney gulped down the doubt that was creeping into her decision. Her attraction to Hayden was far beyond the men she had dated over the past five years here in the city. Every time she was around him, all she wanted to do was re-enact their saucy tryst. He was dangerously handsome and although she knew it was going to be hard seeing him every day; she didn't exactly have any other good options right now. Plus, he was so earnest with his generous offer, which was so sweet. If she was going to do this, she would just have to keep things light, casual, and polite. *Yes, that's what I'm going to do. That and look for a place of my own as soon as possible.*

Grabbing her laptop off her desk, she took a seat at

her kitchen table and searched up flights to Winnipeg. As she booted up her computer, she noticed a notification that she had an unread email. Clicking on the email, she stopped, her body turning ice cold at the sender.

The email read: *You and I belong together, even if you don't think we do. No one can stop true love. Wait for me, baby. We will have our time again. Don't hide from me, bitch. I will always find you.*

"Paul." she whispered. Rising from the table, she paced, her heart racing and the muscles in her body tightened with tension, her telltale sign of an impending panic attack. Knowing what was coming, she sprinted to the door to check her locks, making sure the chain and deadbolt were engaged. She leaned against the door, her throat constricting painfully as she tried to breathe and slid to the floor. Closing her eyes, she willed herself to take deep cleansing breaths, trying to concentrate on controlling the building attack, fighting to take control of her body.

Shortly after she married Paul, she started having panic attacks. At times, they were so debilitating that she couldn't function, and Paul didn't have sympathy for her. He would angrily taunt or make fun of her temporary impairment. Always telling her she was just being stupid or overly dramatic. His unkind words still hurt. Even after so much therapy and healing over the past five years, how did Paul have the ability, with a single email, to make her fold in on herself?

Painful tears wet her cheeks as she held her head in her hands. *What am I going to do? What if Paul is going to show up at my door or at work again? What if the harassment picks up where it left off? What if worse?* Whitney didn't trust

Paul. He was a volatile and unpredictable man, and she simply couldn't and wouldn't go through it all again. Hopeless and scared, she cried, letting all the hurt and fear come out in her sobs.

Wiping her cheeks with her palms, a momentary thought passed through her mind, giving her the strength to rise to her feet and locate her phone. Finding her phone next to her laptop, she quickly typed out a text. *"Can you come get me from the airport tomorrow?"*

CHAPTER 3

*H*ayden arrived at the Winnipeg airport, parking in the car park and finding his way inside. Locating the domestic arrivals, he waited for Whitney, leaning against the wall and watching the empty escalator descend. Being a late-night flight, the terminal was quieter than usual with only a dozen or so loved ones lingering, waiting for the next flight to arrive. Hayden's phone vibrated in his pocket, and he pulled it out, glancing at his texts.

Whitney: Just arrived.

Stuffing his phone back into his pocket, his brows knit together with worry. Receiving a text last night from Whitney, asking if she could come stay with him earlier than planned, he was surprised at her urgency to get there. He wanted to ask what the rush was, but since Whitney was so private, he was hesitant to question it. *Would she trust me enough to even tell me?* Something was obviously very wrong, and he needed to figure out the best way to ask.

The arrival door opened, breaking him out of his thoughts, as passengers started flooding the escalator, descending to the ground floor. Spotting her blonde hair, he smiled, his heart fluttering as warmth filled his chest. Whitney was dressed comfortable and casual in a turquoise fitted athletic jacket, and black leggings, her shoulder-length blonde hair pinned at the sides and her face natural. *Beautiful.* Walking her way, their eyes met, and she offered him a tired and wary smile, causing his stomach to drop. *Something is definitely wrong.*

Whitney stopped a foot from Hayden, staring up at him, trepidation in her eyes. Concern washing over him, he stretched his arms out to her, and she bridged the gap, wrapping her arms around his waist in a tight grip. Melting into his body; a long-pained sigh escaping her lips as she clung to him. He held her to his chest, stroking her hair gently, her tension easing under his tender touch.

Releasing him, she stepped back and met his worried gaze as a grateful smile emerged. "Thank you, Hayden." she said, emotion edging her tone.

"It's no problem, Whitney." he replied, waving off her thanks. "Let's get your luggage and head home." He suggested, walking towards the baggage claim.

Finding one suitcase, she pulled it off the baggage carousel and rolled it over to Hayden. Pulling up the handle, he turned to roll away, and she stopped him with a laugh. "Hold on, I got two more."

Hayden's eyes widened and his lips turned up in a mischievous grin. "Moving in with me already?" he teased with a wink.

Whitney rolled her eyes and shook her head as she went back to the carousel. Retrieving the last two suitcases, she pulled them along awkwardly towards Hayden, who had already commandeered a trolley. Loading up her three suitcases, they made their way out of the building and towards the parkade. It was getting colder now, November just around the corner, and the wind bit at them as they walked.

"My goodness it's cold!" she exclaimed, pulling up the collar of her jacket. "I hope I packed warm enough for Manitoba."

"Winter is coming. You'll need something a lot warmer than that," he informed gesturing to her athletic jacket.

She gave him a sideways glance and shivered, sliding her hands in her pockets. When they reached his truck, Whitney's eyes widened, and she turned, giving Hayden an approving nod. "I love your truck," she marvelled, running her hands over the hardware store logo on the door of his classic Green 1950 Chevy Pickup.

"Thanks, it was my dad's." Hayden answered with a proud smile as he opened the passenger door for her. Flashing him a grateful look, she climbed in.

Loading the suitcases into the bed of the truck, he covered them with a tarp and secured them with bungee cords before returning the trolley. Sliding into the cab, he started the truck and turned to Whitney. She met his gaze, making him melt inside, her cheeks and nose tinted red from the cold. He reached down to turn on the heater, letting the warm air circulate a few minutes before they set on their way. An awkward silence fell between them, neither knowing exactly what to say as they let the cab of the truck warm.

"Better?" he asked, glancing over at her.

"Yes, but my hands are so cold," she replied, rubbing her hands together to generate warmth.

Reaching over to the glove compartment, his hand brushed her thigh, and she raised an eyebrow at him. Chuckling at her reaction, he opened the compartment and pulled out a pair of leather gloves. "These should help." He said, offering them to her.

Her brown eyes softened as she met his gaze and accepted the gloves, slipping them onto her small hands. "These are huge." She commented with a giggle as she held them up, her little hands swimming in his large gloves.

"You know what they say about guys with big hands? They have…" She flashed him a chiding look. "… big gloves." he finished giving her a flirtatious wink and sexy smirk.

Whitney took off a glove and swatted his arm with it, causing them both to laugh. "Enough jokes, country boy! Take me back to Primrose."

An hour later they pulled into the driveway of Hayden's home, and he pressed the button of the garage door opener allowing them to park inside. He turned the truck off and pivoted to Whitney. Halfway through the drive, she had fallen asleep. Her head off to the side of the leather backrest, she looked peaceful. Not having the heart to wake her yet, he took her in. She was so incredibly beautiful, with long dark lashes, perfectly arched eyebrows, a slightly turned-up nose and full lips that begged to be kissed. She was everything he was attracted to, everything he desired, and she was now here with him. He reached over and gently caressed her cheek with the back of his hand, making her stir, then open her brown eyes meeting his gaze. "You feel asleep, gorgeous."

"Oh, sorry." she apologized, sitting up quickly and looking around. "Are we here?"

"Yes," he replied as he climbed out and rounded the truck to the passenger's side, opening her door. She offered him an appreciative grin and slid out of the cab.

Reaching around the truck bed, he unfastened the bungee cords, removed the tarp, and lifted out her luggage. Grabbing two of the largest ones, he carried them in through a side garage door that led straight into the house. Whitney grabbed her lighter bag along with her carry on and followed him inside.

"Home sweet home," he announced, leading her down a short hall into the kitchen. She looked around. The kitchen was modern with stainless steel appliances and beautiful finishes. A long quartz countertop island housed four chairs perfect for casual dining.

"This is nice," she said, eyes darting around the kitchen. She peeked around the corner through the cased opening which led into a large cozy living room.

"Follow me," he gestured. "I'll show you to your room."

"Wow, you're like a full-service bellhop!" she laughed.

"And you don't even need to tip me," he volleyed as he led her through the living room, front entrance and down a long hallway, stopping at a door at the end of the hall.

Putting down one of her suitcases, he opened the door leading her into a large bedroom with a 4-poster king size bed dressed beautifully in a homemade quilt. The quilt was thick and plush in different shades of purple stitched into a star pattern. Whitney put down her suitcase and carry-on bag and went up to the bed, running her hands over the quilt, admiring the handiwork.

"This is beautiful." She commented, tracing the pattern with her fingertips.

Hayden smiled nostalgically. "My mother made it. She always loved to quilt."

"How long has it been since your mother passed away?" she asked, knowing a little about his family from Ever.

"Almost 4 years ago." He replied, as she offered him a sympathetic smile and took a seat on the bed. "My mom and dad passed away in a car accident." He continued. "It was all very sudden, but I'm happy they left this world together. They were inseparable even at the end." Whitney met his eyes and gave him a half smile as he added. "If you're lucky enough to find someone you love and are best friends with, it would be hard to go on without them."

"That would be difficult." She agreed, her eyes downcast as she took in his words.

The air around them growing heavy, Hayden surveyed the bedroom and asked. "Is this room okay for you? There's a huge ensuite bathroom through there." he gestured to the door on the side. "I figured I would you give my bedroom, so you have more space and privacy if you need it."

"Oh, was this your room?" she asked, rising from the

bed, slipping off her tennis shoes and climbing back on, folding her legs in a crisscross.

"Yes, but you can have it. I moved myself just down the hall, two doors down if you need anything."

"Seriously, Hayden." she replied, meeting his gaze with sincerity. "You didn't need to go to that much trouble for me. I know I sprang this impromptu trip on you only last night."

"It's not a big deal, Whitney. I wanted you to be comfortable," he replied, slowly approaching the bed where she sat. Leaning against the bedpost, he cocked his head to the side. *Here's your chance.* "Speaking of that, when we chatted yesterday evening you made it sound like you would be here in a week. Then I got the text that you were hopping the earliest flight you could get out of Toronto. Did something happen?" he asked curiously, putting his hands up in the air. "Only if you want to tell me, Whitney. If you're not comfortable sharing, I'll understand."

Whitney let out a long, shaky exhale and replied. "I guess you could say that I got a little spooked."

"About what?" he asked, furrowing his eyebrows in concern.

"My past seems to be resurfacing out of nowhere.", she replied cryptically.

Hayden rounded the bed post and sat down on the edge of the bed turning his gaze to her. "Your ex-husband?"

Whitney's eyes widened and her face turned white. "How did you know I was married?" she asked pointedly.

"Ben mentioned something about it to me at the

wedding," he confessed. "Was it a secret? Should I not know about it?"

Whitney shook her head. "No, it's fine. It's not like I hide it; I just prefer not to talk about it. It was a dark time in my life."

Hayden pinned her with his gaze, the wall she had erected between them evident and understandable with her past. He reached out and took her hand in his, smoothing over her thumb with his. It was a tender and affectionate gesture, and she glanced down at his hand on hers, then back up to meet his eyes. "I'm sure you'll tell me more about everything later, but for now, get some rest. You must be exhausted," he said, letting go of her hand as he got up from the bed and made his way over to the bedroom door before glancing back at her. "I'm just two doors down if you need me," he reminded her with a waggle of his eyebrows.

Whitney let out her giggle and rolled her eyes at him. "You promised me you would be good."

"I'm just saying this is a full-service establishment," he deadpanned cheekily. "Seriously, anything you need. A cup of sugar, an orgasm. I'm your guy!"

Whitney climbed off the bed and grabbed her shoe, throwing it at him playfully, the shoe hitting him square in the back as he exited the room. He peeked around the door frame, a devilish smile on his face. "Two doors down gorgeous!"

"Get out of here," she giggled, charging the door, and closing it behind him.

CHAPTER 4

$\mathcal{W}$hitney woke up warm and cozy in the big four-poster bed. The handmade quilt was so soft and comfortable she dared not move to disrupt her cocoon of warmth. Raising her head off her pillow, she glanced at her bedside clock, 10:36 a.m. She'd slept in. After such an impulsive departure, she knew her email was probably full of concerned messages responding to a group email she sent out yesterday morning as she quickly packed for this trip. Sending emails to her family, friends, and work colleagues, she couldn't help but smile at the wonderful and supportive people she had in her life.

In the years she was with Paul, he'd slowly isolated her from everyone else. He didn't like her friends, so many of her high school and college friends simply floated away. Then her younger brother joined the RCMP, met his wife and settled on the East Coast. Her father retired from a long career as a detective with the Toronto Police Service and her mother, a retired psychology professor from the

University of Toronto, started enjoying their retirement down south in Arizona during the winter months. So, after her marriage finally ended, she was left with no one. Ever was one of the first female friends she had made since she left her marriage, and her friendship meant everything to Whitney.

Unraveling herself from the warm quilt, Whitney fished out her toiletry bag from her suitcase and padded into the bathroom. The bathroom was nicely renovated with a huge walk-in shower, a long counter with double sinks and plenty of space and a gorgeous free-standing tub. Deciding to take a shower, she stripped off her flannel pajamas and stepped inside, putting on the rain shower setting to help her relax. She stood under the shower for a long time, simply clearing her thoughts so she could start her day. *Breathe in, breathe out,* she let the warm water run over her as a sense of calm flowed through her and any tension in her body dissipated. Feeling sufficiently relaxed, she washed her hair and body, then wrapped herself in a fluffy towel. Entering the bedroom, she heaved a suitcase onto the bed and unzipped it, searching for something comfortable to wear. She chose a warm University of Toronto sweatshirt and her favorite pair of faded jeans, set them on the bed and dropped her towel. Glancing to the side at her reflection in the full-length mirror of the closet, she turned to face it, taking in her body. Standing five feet five, she was slender and toned from years of yoga. Her breasts were still perky and her backside firm and high. She liked the way she looked and thought she looked pretty good for a woman in her mid thirties. Dressing, she could feel her body sigh at the feel of her favorite clothes, and she closed her eyes a moment to take in the blissful feeling of comfort. Returning to the bathroom, she dried her hair, applied some moisturizer, and pulled back half her hair into a makeshift bun at the top of her head. Slipping into a pair of purple fuzzy slippers, she opened her bedroom door and glanced down the hallway now lit with natural light. The bathroom door to her left was open and Hayden's bedroom door was closed. Stopping at his door, she listened, not hearing anything. *Was he still asleep?* Making her way slowly through the house, she curiously surveyed the pictures on the wall and books on the shelves, then entered the kitchen. On the island lay a note and a pink bakery box. The note said:

"Good morning, Whit! I'm just at Prairie Sky doing the morning chores for Ben. I'll be back around noon. I picked up some of the Eazy Café's famous cinnamon buns and made you some coffee. I hope you slept well."

Feeling her stomach rumble, Whitney lifted the lid of the bakery box to the most glorious smell of fresh baked cinnamon buns smothered in cream cheese icing. She combed the cupboards for a plate and utensils, finding what she needed. Lifting one of the large decadent confections out of the box, she eagerly bit into it, the tender pastry, spicy cinnamon, brown sugar, rich cream cheese, and butter enveloping her senses. She closed her eyes, savoring that first perfect bite.

"Dear God, these are orgasmic." she mumbled, opening her eyes, only to be met with a steely blue gaze staring at her from across the island.

"If I knew that was going to be your reaction, I would

have got you these earlier." Hayden commented, a look of pure amusement on his face.

Whitney felt her blush bloom and offered him a sheepish grin, her mouth still full of the delicious treat and a dollop of icing on the tip of her nose. He shook his head and rounded the island, sauntering up to her side and coming dangerously close to her face. Eyes never leaving hers, he drew his hand up and swiped the dollop of frosting off her nose with his index finger. Bringing the finger to his mouth, he sucked it in, then removed his digit with a pop.

"Delicious." he said low and deep, mere inches from her face. Then, with a wicked grin, he turned and strode off towards the bedroom, leaving Whitney speechless.

Whitney's eyes followed him till he was out of sight, and she shook her head, trying to get her wits about her. *Hayden is all your desires personified and now I am living with him in his home. What on earth was I thinking?*

Shifting her attention to the smell of brewed coffee, she poured herself a cup, inhaling the bitter aroma and took a sip. Letting the heat warm her insides, she let out a big sigh. If she was going to live in this house with him for the next few weeks, she needed to set some ground rules with him. *Maybe write them down?* She shook her head. *There is no rule book for this!* All she knew was she needed to keep him at arm's length so she wouldn't be tempted and give into his overtures. Even if her heart wanted to throw out the rule book.

* * *

HAYDEN GRABBED a new pair of jeans and a Henley and threw them onto the bed, choosing something comfortable for a casual Sunday. With the hardware store closed on Sundays, he always enjoyed a quiet day free from responsibility. He would turn on a movie or a hockey game, whatever was on and now, whatever Whitney wanted to watch. Having her in his home was strange but nice, her simple presence changing the air in the house and making his home feel more complete. A feeling he had not felt since his parents passed.

Losing his parents was by far one of the most difficult things he had ever gone through. Being extremely close to them both, especially his mother, not seeing them every day left a huge void in his life. Having worked with his father at their family hardware store since he was a teen, he was suddenly faced with the challenge of running a business, choosing to keep the store as a legacy to his parents. He was grateful everyday for Ben's business savvy in managing the finances for his business. Not having attended college or university, all he knew was the store, so the thought of running his parents' store into bankruptcy was a real worry for him. Together they were able to keep it going and thriving, Ben the business guru and Hayden the expert in product and customer service.

Slipping into the bathroom, he took a quick shower, washing the barn smell from his hair and body and wrapping a towel securely around his waist. Leaving the bathroom, a cloud of steam wafted into the hallway as he turned only to walk right into Whitney. Her hands came up instinctively, bracing herself on his bare chest, and his hands naturally reached for her waist. Her brown eyes were wide with surprise, they slowly drifted up to meet his. *I could take a swim in those eyes.* They were the most beautiful rich brown, like milk chocolate. *Delicious.* His eyes twinkled in amusement as his lips turned up in a playful grin.

Boldly, her eyes grazed over his muscular chest and down to his six-pack just above the towel, before shaking her head and pushing herself away from him, breaking his hold on her waist.

"Sorry." she apologized, that all too familiar rosy blush settling on her cheeks.

Their eyes locked. He ached to touch her face and feel the heat under his hands. She was so cute when she got flustered and he knew it didn't take much to get her there. She diverted her eyes from his, tucked a strand of hair that escaped her bun behind her ear, and shuffled past him, disappearing into her room, and locking the door behind him. He frowned, unsure of how to respond, yet knowing the last thing he wanted to do was make living with him uncomfortable. If he had a fighting chance with Whitney, he needed to be the gentleman he promised he would be.

* * *

WHITNEY CLOSED the door to her room and flipped the lock, resting her back against the door, her breaths coming out staccato as her mind drifted to the impossibly sexy man on the other side of the door. She closed her eyes, trying to steady her breaths, but when she did, flashbacks of their hot and steamy night floated into her consciousness. Letting out a frustrated growl, she glanced around the room, needing a distraction. Locating her phone on the bedside table, she grabbed it and climbed onto the bed, crossing her legs. Opening her phone, notification after notification popped up. Ned, several of her colleagues, a few friends, her parents and one from Ever. *What was Ever doing, messaging me on her honeymoon?* Opening her text, it read.

Ever: "Hey Whitney! Ben just informed me that you're in Primrose. Is everything okay? Call me as soon as you get this."

Against her better judgement, Whitney dialed Ever's number.

"Hello!"

"Hey Ever! How's Hawaii?"

"Gorgeous!" she exclaimed, immediately turning the tables. "I'll tell you all about it later! Why are you in Primrose? Did something happen?"

Whitney lay back on the pillows and sighed. "It's a long story, but in a nutshell, Ned is retiring, the agency is closing, my ex resurfaced, and I'm considering moving to Manitoba."

"Oh wow! That's a lot of change. Ben said you're staying with Hayden."

"For now, yes, he offered, and I needed a place quickly. I intended to fly out closer to when you and Ben returned, but I panicked when Paul started contacting me, so here I am," she explained. "My restraining order expired recently and now he has texted and emailed me. I know I've not shared a lot about him with you, but Paul is unpredictable. I needed to get out of the city quickly."

"Whitney, I can't even imagine." Ever empathized. "Hayden kind of saved the day, then?"

"I guess he did." she sighed. "I'm not sure what I would have done without the offer, honestly. Even after all these years, Paul still scares me."

"Hayden is a good man, Whitney." Ever offered. "He won't let anything happen to you. Does he know the reason you returned to Primrose so quickly? Does he know about Paul?"

"He asked me about it yesterday and I just told him a short version." She answered solemnly.

"Honestly, I think you should tell him, Whitney. Hayden is a great listener."

Whitney rolled her eyes and let out a big guffaw. "You mean when he's not flirting, poking fun and all around flustering me?"

"Seriously Whitney, give him a chance." Ever suggested a little laugh escaping. "He only does those things because he really likes you. You challenge him and I don't think he's used to it. If you ask me, you make him nervous."

"Me?" she questioned. "I highly doubt that."

Ever laughed again. "Yes, you! You have no idea the effect you have on him." She explained. "You are smart, sassy, successful, and beautiful. Hayden is completely smitten with you. Don't you see it?"

Whitney lay back down, looking at the ceiling, her internal dialogue going into overdrive. *Did Hayden really think of me that way? Was he as affected by me as I am affected by him? Why am I asking myself these questions? He couldn't feel the same way. He's just a playboy. He isn't smitten with me. I'm just a conquest.* She groaned at her negative thoughts of

Hayden and reflected on his sweet words about his parent's relationship last night. He spoke with such reverence about them, his admiration for their love and commitment to each other clear. Maybe he wasn't the playboy she thought he was. Maybe he had more depth and did want something more meaningful. One thing she couldn't deny was their crazy chemistry. Like two magnets drawn together. Unable to stay away. And yet she had her doubts.

"Are you sure he likes me that much? I mean, Hayden is just a lot, all the time."

Ever let out a huge guffaw. "I know exactly what you mean! He's Ben's brother, and the apple doesn't fall far from the tree. The Hastings men can be intense. But in the best possible way. Trust me on this, Whitney. Hayden is completely enamoured with you."

Whitney laughed nervously and slapped her hand to her face, not believing what she was about to tell her friend. "So, you know the night of your gallery opening?" she asked, internally wincing at the confession that was about to spew out of her mouth.

"Yes."

"Hayden and I kind of slept together." she blurted out, throwing her arm over her eyes.

"I knew it!" Ever exclaimed excitedly.

Whitney sat up again, crossing her legs. "What do you mean, you knew? Did Hayden say something to Ben?" Whitney questioned; eyebrows raised.

"No, no, nothing like that. C'mon, Whitney, you must admit, you two have a noticeable sexual energy with each other. Even Bea noticed it at the wedding."

Whitney's eyes closed, and she took a deep breath. "Had it really been that obvious?" she asked, curling up her nose, a small smile tugging at her lips.

"To us, yes, but we know you both. To everyone else, the chemistry was cracking all over the place." She shared. "I promise you; he's not the player you think he is. Would it be so bad to get to know him more? Maybe go on a few dates?"

"No, I guess not." Whitney conceded. *It wouldn't be bad at all.*

* * *

HAYDEN SAT on the couch flipping through channels. Whitney had been in her bedroom for the last two hours. *What is she doing? Napping, reading, working? Maybe she's too embarrassed by our hallway encounter or frustrated with me and she wanted to be alone?* The thought of that troubled him. He had always tried to be good to the women he was interested in or dated, and even though some people labelled him a player, he knew that label was the farthest thing from the truth. He was a one-woman kind of man, always giving his full attention to one woman at a time. *Is it my problem that none of them lasted?* All he wanted was what Ben had found. *Is that too much to ask?* Yes, he had a business that was doing well; he had friends; he had his brother and now Ever, but he wanted the love of a good woman. A woman that would appreciate his sense of humour, his strong work ethic and challenge him in life. His best friend, but also a passionate lover. Someone he could laugh with, have serious conversations with and couldn't go a day without touching, kissing, and holding in his arms. Someone who someday would help him create a family of his own. Visions of Whitney's beautiful face clouded his thoughts, and he smiled. *Whitney could be that woman.* The question was, would she let him in?

"Hockey fan?" a soft voice asked from behind him, breaking him from his revery.

His eyes flitting up to the screen to the hockey game he had stopped on and he glanced behind him to see Whitney, leaning against the frame of the cased opening to the living room, hands clasped in front of her.

"Yeah, you?" he asked, his eyes following her as she rounded the side of the couch.

She sat down at the other end, curled her fluffy slipper feet under her and gave him a warm smile. "I am. My brother used to play, and I always enjoyed watching with my dad," she answered, putting her focus on the game. "I've never actually been to an NHL game, though."

He smiled, taking her in, looking casual and cozy, in her University of Toronto sweatshirt and faded blue jeans. The kind of jeans that hugged her curves perfectly and looked well worn and loved. Her favorite pair, he assumed. She was so naturally beautiful, with no makeup. *Are those freckles on her nose?* He groaned internally; she was so gorgeous it made his chest hurt.

"Are you going to just sit there and stare at me or are you going to watch the game?" she asked, giving him a sideways glance, an amused smile tugging on her lips.

"I was thinking a little of both," he answered with a laugh as he got up from the couch and strode into the kitchen. Retrieving a bag of potato chips from the cupboard, he poured them into a bowl and opened the refrigerator. "Beer?" he asked.

"Sure!" she exclaimed, nestling deeper into the couch.

He pulled out two bottles and made his way back to the living room, along with the bowl of chips. Settling the bowl between them, he handed her a bottle. She twisted the top off and took a long, rather impressive swig, making him smile in surprise and admiration.

"Hits the spot." She shrugged, holding out her beer bottle to clink his. Hayden obliged with a laugh and settled back into the couch.

They watched for a while, making comments on players, sharing their favorite teams and player stats. She knew her hockey, and he was thoroughly impressed.

"We'll have to go to a game sometime." He offered, waiting to see her reaction.

She turned to him, a cheeky grin on her face as she asked. "Are you asking me out on a date, Hays?"

"I believe I am Whit," he replied, matching her smile.

"Sure.", she replied, reaching over, and grabbing a handful of chips, then making a show of popping one into her mouth.

Hayden chuckled and shook his head. Whitney had just given him an in, and he wasn't going to squander this opportunity.

CHAPTER 5

Over the next week, they settled into a routine with each other. Hayden would get up early, making Whitney coffee and breakfast before he left to chore the animals at Prairie Sky, and then he would open the store, working until late afternoon, at which time his evening staff would take over. Whitney had scheduled meetings with several Winnipeg artists and with Ben and Ever away, she borrowed Ever's car so she could meet with her clients. She was always dressed to the nines, in killer suits and heels, looking like the professional she was. Although she looked stunning, Hayden liked her most at home in her favorite sweatshirt and jeans, sans makeup, reading on the couch with her sexy librarian glasses on, watching hockey with him, or at the island enjoying a piece of pizza as she laughed at his jokes.

On Friday he came home, as usual, hanging up his keys at the back door and making his way into the kitchen, hoping to see Whitney sitting at the island with her laptop, as she usually did. Not there. He glanced into the living room and a sly smile curled his lips. There she was, downward dog, her amazing backside high in the air. He tilted his head, admiring her rear end, watching her transition into a warrior pose, then into a wheel pose. He knew a little about yoga having taken a beginner class at the Primrose Community Centre. Of course, the only reason he took the class was because he thought it might be a good place to meet women. Turns out all he met were all the ladies from the fifty-five plus Senior Centre. He smiled at the memory of those dirty old birds, hooting and hollering as he did the poses, one giving his butt a hearty pinch. Whitney, still in her wheel pose, opened her eyes to meet his gaze. He grinned at her, his smile stretching ear to ear. "Very bendy," he commented, waggling his eyebrows at her flirtatiously.

She smiled as she lowered herself to her yoga mat and lay there a moment, taking several deep breaths before sitting up, bowing her namaste and reaching for her water bottle. "How long were you watching me?" she asked, pivoting herself to face him, her legs still crossed on her mat.

"Long enough." he smirked, leaning both of his elbows casually against the island.

Whitney shook her head and giggled as she asked. "Do you always have sex on the brain?"

"Yeah, pretty much," he answered honestly, striding over to her, and putting out his hand to help her up.

Shaking her head again, she accepted his offered hand, letting him pull her up. Hayden took that moment to check her out fully and liking very much what he saw. A purple bra top displaying her gorgeous curves and toned midriff and black yoga shorts showing off her toned and shapely legs. Her body was on full display, and he was in awe. "Whit, seriously, your body is incredible," he complimented.

Whitney smiled, a blush forming on her cheeks, as she took a seat at the island next to him. "Thank you." She said. "Yoga is a lifesaver. I'm a chronic overthinker and get anxious, so it helps calm my mind."

"I can see that," he commented, backtracking to clarify. "I mean, I'm pretty sure I figured that out about you already."

"Sorry, I know I'm too much." She said with a wince as she curled up her nose.

He reached for her hand and took it in his, giving it a gentle squeeze. "No gorgeous, you're just enough."

A smile curved her lips as she took in his sweet compliment. She turned her body to face him and took both of his hands, lacing her fingers with his. He glanced down at their hands, loving the way they looked together. His, large and thick, and hers, small and dainty. Her eyes drifted up to meet his gaze as she rose from her stool, searching his eyes, her hand coming up and smoothing down his hair affectionately. Her gaze softened with appreciation as she took his face between her hands and brushed her lips gently to his.

His heart fluttered wildly in his chest, and he kissed her back, matching her tenderness. They broke apart, and he looked deep into her eyes, now glistening with unshed tears.

"Thank you." She whispered with an emotional crack

in her voice, which made his heart instantly ache. Releasing his hands, she pivoted and strode off towards the bedrooms, her hand touching her cheek to catch a stray tear.

Hayden sat there dumbstruck at what had just happened. He touched his lips, still tingling from her unexpected kiss. *What has she been through? Who made her feel like she was not enough?* Hayden needed to find out. He needed to hear her story. In his eyes, Whitney was perfect, and he was determined to show how much he cared for her.

* * *

WHITNEY ROLLED out of bed and stretched, yawning deeply. Since she had come to Primrose, she had slept better and deeper than she had in her entire life. Maybe it was all the clean air, maybe it was that for the first time in years, she didn't have to rush into the office. Maybe it was the feeling of contentment her current living arrangement was giving her. It had been exactly one week today since she came to Primrose, and Hayden had been so sweet to her. He was attentive to her needs and always greeted her with a big smile, like he was incredibly happy to see her every day. She anticipated seeing him each morning, the conversation they shared and even their flirtatious banter. Then there was yesterday, his sincere words touching her deeply. She sat back down on her bed and sighed. No one had ever told her she was enough. Something she had longed so deeply to hear from her ex-husband, flowed so freely from Hayden. Staring into his eyes, she could see his genuine feelings for her, and it made her heart swell. Hayden was breaking through, and she could feel her walls slowly coming down. Brick by brick.

Whitney showered, dressed, and put on some light makeup. Having heard his shower earlier, she knew Hayden was up and probably watching TV as he sipped on his morning coffee. Exiting her room, she heard music; the sound growing louder as she made her way down the hall. Rounding the corner of the living room, she stopped in her tracks and a slow smile curled her lips. "Jump" by Van Halen blasted from mobile speakers filling the house with guitar riffs and sharp drumbeats as a shirtless Hayden dressed only in faded low-slung jeans, shook his hips to the music and sang, rather terribly into the turner he held in his hand. She stifled a laugh as he hit the high notes and flipped an egg he'd been cooking in the frying pan on the stove. Hayden turned, his handsome smile growing wider when he spotted her and lifted his makeshift microphone to his lips, then sang at the top of his lungs.

"Might as well jump! JUMP!"

Whitney lost it, keeling over with laughter as he rounded the island and offered her a wooden spoon. Gesturing for her to sing with him, she let out a note that was probably not human and shrugged, joining him in the chorus, not caring how tone deaf she sounded. As the song ended, they both laughed hysterically until Hayden noticed his eggs and bacon still on the stove.

"Hungry?" he asked, drawing his attention back to the frying pan.

"Starved." she replied, taking a seat at the island, feeling light and buoyant from their impromptu karaoke session.

"We got eggs, bacon and toast and I already poured you your coffee just the way you like it."

She smiled at how, even after just a short time, he already knew her preferences. Setting a plate in front of her, he paused for a moment, waiting for her to dig in. She picked up a piece of bacon and made a show of taking a bite. "Good," she mumbled with a nod.

"Oh, and I have something for you," he said, his eyes flashing with excitement. Hayden rushed into the little hallway between the garage and kitchen and came back with a dozen red roses in a glass vase and an envelope strategically placed between the stems.

Whitney paused mid bite, putting down her piece of bacon as he placed them in front of her. "Hayden, you didn't need to do this!" she beamed.

"I know, but I wanted to." he smiled sweetly at her. "You deserve flowers every day, Whit. So, let's start with today."

Whitney pushed aside her plate and pulled the vase towards her, burying her nose in the red buds. Taking a deep inhale, she let their sweet smell envelop her. She had always loved red roses, but no one had ever given her any. Even her ex-husband, when they were dating, had never bought her roses. It was like Hayden knew her deepest wishes. Whitney crooked her finger at Hayden and gestured him over to her. He rounded the island and stood in front of her, his coffee mug in hand. She stood up and put her arms around his neck, looking him deep into his eyes. "You are the sweetest." she said as she went on her tiptoes to kiss his lips tenderly.

The feel of his muscular body against her soft curves made her heart flutter and head spin. He set down his mug, wrapped his powerful arms around her waist and pulled her closer, molding their bodies together as he deepened their kiss, the tip of his tongue teasing her lips to open for him. They parted, allowing him entrance as he softly stroked his tongue against hers. A whimper of approval escaped her throat as he kissed her tenderly, but thoroughly. Pulling away breathless; her lips tingled, and her body shivered. He ran his large hands over her arms as if to warm her and kissed her on the head affectionately.

"Are you going to open the envelope?" he asked, gesturing to it still nestled amongst the roses.

She turned, a huge smile on her face, and plucked the envelope from the bouquet. Opening the envelope, she pulled out two tickets to the NHL game for that night. Her eyes widened with excitement, and she let out a squeal, wrapping her arms around him for another hug.

"So, I guess you're a yes to going out tonight?" he laughed at her reaction.

"Heck, yes!" she exclaimed, looking at the tickets in her hands.

"How about dinner and drinks beforehand and then the game?"

"Sounds perfect." She said, settling back down in front of her breakfast.

Her first official date with Hayden. This was a big deal,

and she knew exactly who she was going to call to help her get ready.

* * *

WHITNEY RECRUITED the help of the only other person she knew in Primrose, Beatrix Baxter. Bea, who had the day off work, brought with her some "hockey game appropriate attire" as she called it.

Bea was perched on the bed, feet dangling off the end. She was the definition of petite, but what she lacked in size she made up for in personality.

"Whitney, get your ass out here!"

"I don't know, Bea!" Whitney shouted from the bathroom, apprehension in her tone. "I mean they fit, but they are extremely tight. You're a lot smaller than me."

"Oh, stop! Your body rocks! Show me."

Whitney hesitantly came out of the bathroom and turned to look in the full-length mirror. Taking in her appearance, she was surprised how good she looked.

"Holy crap, you look hot!" Bea exclaimed, hopping off the bed and coming up beside her as she surveyed her reflection in the mirror. "Hayden isn't going to be able to keep the drool in his mouth."

"You think?" Whitney questioned, turning to the side as a smile tugged at her lips.

"I know." Bea answered, nodding her head. "I've known Hayden forever and I'm certain you look like his biggest fantasy right now."

Whitney giggled, turning to Bea. "What's next?"

Rubbing her hands together, Bea flashed Whitney a coy smile. "Hair and makeup, baby."

* * *

Hayden leaned against the island in the kitchen waiting for Whitney, absentmindedly flipping through his phone. The women had been in her room for over an hour, the sounds of their laughter making him curious as to what they were up to. Taking his time getting ready for his date with Whitney, he had been waiting patiently for the past 20 minutes for them to emerge. Finally, he heard the unmistakable sound of the door opening down the hall, accompanied by their giggles. He stood up straight, shoving his phone into his pocket. Bea walked in first, a look of accomplishment on her face. He cocked an eyebrow at his friend as she approached him.

"Wait for it…" she said, a coy smile on her face.

His eyes darted towards the cased opening just as Whitney rounded the corner and his jaw slacked, his mouth instantly dry as his pulse went into overdrive.

"Hot damn," he whispered under his breath, his eyes feasting on her, his head feeling a little woozy as all blood rushed south.

Whitney stood before him, in a tight blue long sleeve scoop neck Winnipeg Jets T-shirt that kissed the top of her ample curves and a pair of dark wash skinny jeans that were so tight, they looked like they were painted onto her body. Her outfit was completed with a pair of brown knee-high low heel boots. Her shoulder-length blonde hair was pulled back at the sides and her makeup was sultry and sexy with smoky eyes rimmed by dark full lashes, making her brown eyes pop and glossed, kissable lips. He was speechless as he took in the sexiest woman he had ever seen.

"Well, folks, my work here is done." Bea said with a laugh, breaking Hayden from his stare. "You two kids have fun tonight!" she exclaimed with a wiggle of her brows as she made her way into the front entrance and saw herself out.

Hayden returned his gaze to Whitney, saliva pooling in his mouth as his eyes raked over her magnificent body.

Whitney glanced down self-consciously and back up to meet his intense gaze. "Are you sure I look, okay?"

He wet his lips and stuttered. "You...you look beyond amazing!" he exclaimed, swallowing down hard. "I'm not sure I want to take you out looking like that. I'll have to beat the men off with a stick."

"Stop." Whitney pleaded, with a giggle as she swatted him with the flannel shirt jacket she was holding.

Hayden grabbed her arm and pulled her into him, settling his hands on her hips. "You are so incredibly beautiful, Whitney." he said as he lifted her chin up to look into his eyes. "You are beautiful every day, with or without makeup, dressed up for work or on the couch in jeans and a sweatshirt. And now in this hot as hell hockey fan get up..." he paused, spinning her around to take a not-so-subtle peek at her backside. "Nope, I take it back. I demand you live in these jeans from now on."

"Hayden, you're ridiculous." She said with a giggle and a roll of her eyes as she put her arms around his torso, giving him a big hug. "I'll take the compliment, though. Thank you."

Hayden folded her into his arms, enjoying how they simply fit, like she was designed just for him. Kissing her on the head, he gave her one last squeeze and released her. "Are you ready to go, gorgeous?"

"Yes, I am!" she replied excitedly, putting on her flannel jacket. "Will this be warm enough?"

"I think so," he offered, reaching for his keys and turning to give her a sly smile. "If not, I'll keep you warm."

Hayden and Whitney made their way along the downtown sidewalk, hand in hand, the bite of the cold winter wind against their faces, promising snow, and a possible storm. They slipped between the doors of the restaurant, and Whitney shivered. As they waited for the hostess to greet them, Hayden rubbed her shoulders to help warm her.

"A table?" the young, willowy blond, statuesque hostess asked as she eyed Hayden up and down and flashed him a flirty smile.

"Yes, for two." Hayden answered, pulling Whitney into him and giving her a tender kiss on the cheek.

The hostess glanced from Hayden to Whitney, a look of disappointment on her face. "Follow me," she directed in an annoyed, monotone voice as she led them to a booth in the corner of the restaurant.

Sliding into the booth across from each other, Hayden immediately took Whitney's hand in his. The hostess flashing them a look of distaste, as she set their menus down, then turned on her heel, and Whitney swore she heard her let out a frustrated huff.

"I think she's a little disappointed." Whitney laughed, her eyes dancing in amusement as she followed the hostess across the restaurant. "She was full on checking you out."

"Not my type." Hayden shrugged, completely indifferent.

"What is your type, anyway?" Whitney asked, leaning toward him, hands folded in front of her.

Hayden met her eyes with a serious look and smiled before replying. "You."

Whitney let out a nervous laugh, then realizing he was being serious, cleared her throat and searched his eyes curiously. "You say that, but you don't really know me all that well yet." Whitney questioned, then added with emphasis, "Like really know me, Hayden."

Leaning back against the booth, he squinted, processing her words. Reaching across the table he took her hand in his, then replied, "I'm more than aware that technically we've not known each other long, but I want to know everything about you, Whitney." he confessed stroking his thumb over hers methodically. "I realize we're going backwards here, having seen each other naked before," he added, giving her a coquettish wink, and making her smile. "But I would like to know more about you, if you're willing to open up to me."

Whitney met his sincere gaze, longing in their depths. Hayden had no agenda other than to get to know her and he had more than proven himself to her. Ever was right. Hayden was trustworthy.

Interrupting their conversation, their waiter took their drink and food orders, then hustled off, letting them continue. The disruption was welcome, giving Whitney more time to think about what she was willing to share with Hayden. "So, what do you want to know?" Whitney asked, leaning back into the plush backrest.

"I'm curious about your history," he confessed. "I know maybe it's something you don't like to talk about, but since I'm serious about getting to know you and what makes you tick; I think you should start there."

"Wow, you're just going for it, aren't you?" she asked, looking away and letting out a nervous giggle.

Hayden shrugged, offering her a smile as he leaned back against the backrest and gestured for her to go ahead.

Whitney leaned forward and folded her hands in front of her, letting out a long, nervous exhale. *How do I go from holding everything in to spilling my guts to a man I'm romantically interested in?* She had held it in so long that she was struggling to formulate the words to start the conversation.

As if reading her mind, Hayden leaned forward and put his hands on hers, the warmth of his touch calming her and letting her know it was okay. "Whitney, you can tell me anything," he assured her. "I won't pass judgement; you can trust me."

Whitney sighed and swallowed hard, feeling a lump of emotion forming. She closed her eyes and took a deep, cleansing breath as she spoke. "I guess I'll start from the beginning." She said in a shaky voice. "I was married for seven years, five together and two legally separated. I got married when I was 23. I met Paul when I was working at a neighbourhood coffee shop and in my last year at university. He would always come in and was sweet and charming. He asked me out every day for months, so I finally said yes, and we started dating. Paul was five years older than me and more experienced in life, but I was completely head over heels for him back then and before I knew it, we were engaged and planning a wedding." She explained. "I moved in with him before we got married and that is when I remember the abuse starting."

"Abuse?" Hayden questioned, contorting his face in disgust. "Did he hit you?"

"No, but sometimes I wish he did." She confessed. "At least if I had cuts or bruises, then I would've had physical proof of his abuse. He was emotionally and mentally abusive towards me." She shared meeting Hayden's eyes. "It started with small comments or criticisms. First, making rude or crude comments about my looks, what I wore, and so on. Then he started isolating me from my friends and limiting my contact with my family. It wasn't until I left him and started going to therapy that I under-stood that those seemingly small things were part of the abuse." Hayden shook his head and encouraged her to continue with a gentle squeeze of his hand. "About two years into our marriage, living with him had become a roller coaster. I asked his sister about his moods, and she shared with me that Paul had been diagnosed with manic depression years prior and that was likely why he had such extreme mood swings. When I found out, I confronted him about it, asking him why he never told me. I asked him simply because I wanted to help him.

Perhaps there was medication, or some type of therapy he could go through that would help. I didn't know." she shrugged. "I even asked my mother about treatment for him as my mother was a Psychology Professor."

"Makes sense." Hayden said. "You loved him and wanted to help him."

"Exactly, or at least, I thought so, but the more I talked about it the worse the abuse got. He would take out his frustration and anger on me by calling me horrible names, attacking my looks, my weight, my character. Nothing was off limits. He couldn't keep a job and started flipping from one career to the next, blaming the reason for his inability to keep a job on me." Hayden shook his head, his mouth setting into a grim line. "Honestly, I don't know how I survived those years; my self esteem was in the toilet." she confessed. "In the last year of our marriage, he started accusing me of cheating on him. If I would say hello to someone while we were out, or stop to talk to a neighbour, he would accuse me of sleeping with them. He was relentless with it, calling me a slut or a whore." Hayden met her gaze with empathy as she continued. "That part was so hard for my young mind at that time. He was my first for everything. He was the only man I had ever slept with and had pledged my love and life to him in marriage. And even with all of that, he didn't believe me." Hayden let out a long breath. "Finally, after five years of dealing with his abuse, he came home one day and told me he was done with me. He said I had one day to get my things out and go."

"What did you do?" Hayden questioned, his eyebrows knitting together as he frowned.

"Well, I called my parents, of course, which was terrifying for me. They had always been unconditionally supportive and did whatever they could to make Paul feel like part of our family. Despite that, I knew they felt Paul was not right for me and could see that things weren't good in my marriage. When I called them, they came, no questions asked." Whitney smiled in reflection. "In some ways, looking back, I think they were relieved that I was leaving him. That I had found my way out of the relationship."

Hayden shook his head again, letting out a long-pained exhale, Whitney sitting back and doing the same as their eyes met.

"I literally have never told anyone that much about those years." she confessed a sense of calm washing over her at sharing her entire story. "Even Ever doesn't know everything."

Hayden intertwined his fingers with hers and glanced down at their joined hands. Leaning over the table, he brought her hand to his lips, planting a kiss on it. "I want you to know I don't take your trust in me for granted," he said, looking deep into her eyes. "I'm so sorry you had to go through all that."

Whitney gave him an appreciative look, then continued. "I've never hidden my past from others, just simply given them the short version when they asked. After Paul and I split, so much stuff came to light. He'd been seeing someone for months behind my back before he asked me to leave, and after that girl broke it off with him, he tried everything to get back together with me," she continued.

"It got to the point of stalking me, so I had to get a restraining order against him."

"And he's been contacting you again?" Hayden asked to clarify. "Doesn't that go against the restraining order?"

"Unfortunately, the restraining order has now lapsed and yes, he has attempted contact." She confirmed. "I really don't know how he got my info. I assume somehow through the agency, as my info is public on the website. But I don't think he knows where I live or anything like that, even though he claimed in his messages that he knows where I am."

Hayden ran his hand through his hair and let out a long breath. "Do you think he's going to try to hurt you in any way?" He asked, a look of worry on his face.

"Physically, I don't think so, but mentally I'm sure of it. His messages so far have been full of insults and his usual name calling."

"So that's the reason you left Toronto so quickly?" Hayden asked, putting two and two together. She nodded and took a drink of her water. Hayden met her gaze, a gentle reassurance on his face. "He's not going to hurt you, Whitney. Not on my watch."

Whitney stared at Hayden. This amazing man sitting across from her promising her his protection. Her heart felt full and a deep sense of peace came over her, making her feel truly safe for the first time in a week.

* * *

AFTER DINNER, they made their way to the arena and found their seats near the home team bench and settled in.

"Wow, Hayden, these are great seats!" Whitney exclaimed excitedly, her eyes darting around, wanting to take everything in.

"Are you okay here for a bit?" he asked with a mischievous wink. "I promise I'll try to be quick."

Whitney nodded and watched him go bounding up the steps two at a time. She relaxed into her seat and took in the view in front of her. The arena was huge, a giant jumbotron over the middle of the ice, flashing stats and info on the players. Music played loudly amongst the chatter of the growing crowd to pump everyone up. The seats in their section were filling up fast and before long, 15 minutes had passed, and Whitney was beginning to worry about where Hayden was. Hayden hadn't been gone long, but she wanted him near her, his simple presence making her feel secure and cared for.

A whistle sounded, and she followed the sound to see three guys sitting in the seats behind her, not there when she and Hayden had arrived. The man in the middle leaned down to her, his breath warm on her hair.

"Hey there, sweetheart. Are you here alone?" he asked, his hand touching her shoulder and lingering unnecessarily.

She flinched from his unwanted touch and turned to give him her fiercest glare.

He put his hands up and laughed. "Don't be so jumpy, sweetheart. Just curious."

"She's with me," a low firm voice sounded as Hayden appeared, two bottles of soda in one hand and a bag from the souvenir shop in the other. Squinting, he gave the men a steely glare as they cowered back in their seats.

Hayden sat down beside her, handing her a bottle of soda, concern etched on his face. "Are you okay?"

"Yes, I'm glad you got back when you did, though." She said, feigning distress. "I was about to unleash a big can of whoop ass on him and I didn't want to get thrown out of my first ever NHL game!"

"I actually would have liked to have seen that!" Hayden laughed as he leaned in and planted a chaste kiss on her lips.

Whitney put her drink in her holder and glanced curiously down at the bag he was holding. Hayden smiled and reached into the bag pulling out a team toque with a large pom pom on top and a pair of matching mittens. "I got you these for you to commemorate your first NHL game, and because you're always cold," he said, putting the toque on her head and helping her into the mittens.

Whitney clapped her mittened hands happily, her brown eyes dancing with delight as she flashed him an appreciative smile. "I love them! But does this mean you aren't going to keep me warm?" she asked, playfully putting her lip out in a pout.

Hayden chuckled, the sound low and sweet as he put his arm around her shoulders, and she snuggled into him.

* * *

THE GAME OVER, their voices hoarse from cheering, Hayden and Whitney followed the crowd out of the arena, laughing and holding hands. Hayden loved how easy it was to be with Whitney. She was fun, silly, and their shared interests were such a welcome surprise to him. Her guard had come down, offering him uninhibited affection, and allowing him to reciprocate. Despite this change, he would not rush their connection, rather savor every bit she offered him and let her take the lead.

Coming into the main lobby, they both glanced out at the street through the floor to ceiling windows. The snow was coming down in giant flakes, soft and plentiful. The visibility even in the middle of downtown was questionable.

"I need to check the road conditions." Hayden commented, his face etched with worry as he took a seat on a nearby bench.

Whitney looked out the window, her brows knitting in concern at the turn in weather.

Hayden pulled up his highway conditions app and winced. "Travel is not recommended."

"What do we do then?" Whitney asked, taking a seat next to him and resting her hand on his thigh.

"Well, we could rent a hotel room." He suggested, his eyebrows raised in question. "But I don't know if you're comfortable with that."

"Hayden, is this your way of spending the night with me?" she teased with a giggle, pointing to the swirling snow outside.

Hayden laughed and put his arm around her. "If only I wielded that type of power, but alas, mother nature is the culprit. There is a hotel just a few blocks from here. Do we chance it out there?" he asked, pointing his thumb behind them, to the winter storm outside.

"I think we can," she said, buttoning up her jacket and slipping on her mittens and toque. "I'm ready."

He smiled and leaned in to kiss her sweetly as he tugged the toque over her eyes. "You are so damn cute!"

She grinned and rose from the bench, grabbing his hand. "Which way?"

He pointed toward the hotel, and they slipped out the large doors into the winter wonderland that was downtown Winnipeg. Hand in hand, they hurried down the street, the snow thick and heavy, coming down on them as they trudged along the sidewalk towards the hotel. Reaching their destination, they entered the lobby and shook off the snow now covering them.

"You two look cold!" the friendly middle-aged woman at the concierge desk commented. "Those Manitoba storms, I tell you. Luckily, this one is supposed to let up tomorrow sometime. Can I get you a room for the night?"

"Yes, please." Hayden replied as they stepped up to the desk and he glanced down at Whitney for clarification, asking, "Or do we need two?"

Whitney met his questioning gaze, and a slow smile curved her lips as she turned to answer the concierge, "One room, please."

Hayden smiled back, feeling a pang of anticipation, his heart pounding hard in his chest. They had bridged a gap tonight, and she was choosing to let him in.

"Perfect," the woman commented as she checked them in and, after explaining the amenities, handed Hayden the key cards.

Making their way to the elevator, Whitney reached out and intertwined her fingers with Hayden's. He glanced at Whitney, thinking he would see her hesitation, but when she met his inquiring gaze all he saw was her consent. Reaching their floor, they quickly found their room and opened the door. The room was large with a king size bed in the middle, a long desk, with a TV above it and a chair by the large floor to ceiling window.

Removing their jackets, they went to work on their boots, Whitney struggling to remove hers. "Let me help you," he offered, gesturing for her to have a seat on the bed.

She sat, leaned back on her elbows and let him remove one boot, then unzip the second and pulled that one off as well. Putting her boots by the front entrance, he returned and knelt in front of her to rub her feet and calves, his eyes transfixed on hers.

Whitney let out a moan of satisfaction as he massaged her instep. Letting her head fall back as she relaxed under his touch. Hayden smiled, deciding tonight was going to be all about her. She deserved to be worshipped, and he was going to show her how wonderful it was to be with someone that truly cherished her. Whitney lifted her head, her beautiful brown eyes blazing with desire. Sitting up, she took his face in her hands, her voice raspy with need. "I want you, Hayden."

"I want you too, Whitney." he replied, the intense heat between them sparking like firecrackers.

She ran her hands through his hair, tugging at it playfully, making his breath catch as she breathed out the words he had waited to hear. "Make love to me tonight."

Eyes locked on hers, Hayden rose to his feet, taking her hand and pulling her up to join him. Running his hands over her sides, his fingertips found the hem of her shirt as he slowly lifted it over her head and tossed it towards the chair by the window. She wore a black lace bra that barely held her perfect curves. He ran his large hands over her arms and up her sides, before tangling them in her hair, pulling her into him for a long, languid kiss. The kiss was deep and sensual, and his groin tightened as their embrace heated. Parting her lips, she let his tongue explore her mouth, showing her without words everything he wanted to do to her tonight. She moaned sweetly, and he swallowed her moan with his lips. Reaching behind him, he pulled his sweatshirt over his head, baring himself to her. She flashed him a look of approval as she ran her hands over his muscles, mapping each edge and angle with her fingertips. He closed his eyes, reveling in the feel of her touch. He reached behind her and unclasped her bra, letting it fall to the floor. Her pert breasts were full and soft, peaked with rosy nipples made his mouth water. He looked down at her, so vulnerable and trusting, half naked in front of him. He had never seen a woman more beautiful than Whitney Faris.

"Lay back on the bed, gorgeous." He ordered softly as he got down on his knees in front of her and reached for the button on her jeans. "Let me help you out of these."

Whitney let out a sharp giggle, remembering how hard they were to put on. "Good luck," she replied. "They're extremely tight."

"Oh, I noticed," he confirmed with a husky laugh. "But damn, they're sexy."

Whitney smiled up at him as he unzipped the fly and eased them over her hips and down her toned legs, coming off with shocking ease. His wanton gaze raked over her body as his eyes settled on the black lace thong and the treasure that awaited within.

"Your turn," she whispered, meeting his hungry gaze. He unbuttoned his jeans and removed them, then lowered his boxers, freeing himself from their restraint.

* * *

WHITNEY'S EYES roamed down Hayden's magnificent body, unapologetically taking in every inch of powerful perfection. Her core pulsed in anticipation of the pleasure she knew he could bring her as she grew wet with wanton need. Reaching down, he hooked his thumbs under the sides of her thong and slowly removed them, leaving her bare.

"Slide up on the bed," he ordered, his voice low and sexy. She shimmied herself till she was in the middle, and he climbed onto the bed, coming over her, the heat of his body scorching her skin as he hovered above her with his strong arms. Whitney loved the feel of his body on hers and her breath caught as she felt his hardness between them. Capturing her lips, he kissed her long and deep, the sensual feel of his tongue caressing hers driving her wild.

"I want you to feel good tonight," he said between deliciously passionate kisses. "Just tell me what you like, okay?"

Abandoning her lips, he planted hot kisses down her neck, making her skin raise with goosebumps. His tongue traced the hollow of her throat, which unexpectedly caused a bolt of sensation between her legs. A newfound erogenous zone. She writhed beneath his touch as he licked his way down to her breast and gently massaged it taking the nipple into his mouth. He sucked it gently at first, grazing the peak with his teeth, then sucked harder, making her core quiver with pleasure.

"Hayden, that feels so good," she panted, giving in to the desire he was creating.

He worshipped one breast, then the other until she was teetering so close to the edge she wanted to cry. Rubbing his thumb over her taut nipple. He sucked it in again, circling it with his tongue as he played with the other sensitive peak, causing her to moan and bow off the bed as pleasure rolled through her body. Continuing his attention on her breasts, he reached between her legs, massaging the soft folds drenched from her desire. She parted her legs, allowing him access as he dragged out her climax, making her legs shake from the intensity. Coming down from her high, she turned, meeting him with hazy lust drunk eyes.

"That was beautiful," he said, staring at her with reverence. "Have you ever been able to orgasm that way?"

She shook her head. Her experience in the bedroom was, in one word, limited. "I haven't exactly had that much experience," she confessed, transfixing her gaze on him. "Other than my ex, there has only been you."

Hayden's eyes flashed with surprise at her confession and Whitney turned her head, covering her eyes with her arm. "I realize it's strange that I'm 34 and I've only had two sexual partners."

Hayden lifted her arm off her eyes so he could meet them and gave her a sweet smile. "It's not strange, Whitney. You value yourself and your body and you're not willing to give all of you to just anyone. You should be proud of that."

Whitney searched his eyes, seeing he meant each word. Hayden respected her and he wasn't taking their intimacy lightly. *Where did this incredible man come from?* She had been so wrong about Hayden. He wasn't a playboy or just out to bed her. He was selfless, tender, and made her feel truly wanted for the first time in her life. If her experiences had taught her anything, it was that she deserved to be loved and cherished. *Love? Am I falling for Hayden?* Surprised that the word love had floated into her consciousness, she suddenly felt hopeful. Maybe Hayden was that second chance she had hoped to find one day. How he listened to her story tonight and even after sharing everything with him, he still wanted her. It wasn't just about their physical connection anymore. They were now emotionally bonded to one another, and for her, that made tonight a turning point in their relationship.

Whitney shifted towards him, bringing herself closer, and reached down to stroke his manhood. He felt so good in her hands, smooth and hard as steel. "I want you inside me, Hayden. Now, please."

Rolling off the bed, he returned with a condom in his hand.

"Let me," she offered, sitting up and plucking the packet from his fingers. Her eyes never leaving his as she opened the pack with her teeth and pulled out the condom, sliding it down his length with one swift move. He let out a groan at her touch and, once fully sheathed, covered her with his powerful body. Her legs fell open, allowing him to nestle at her apex. Brushing her hair from her face, he looked deep into her eyes, his gaze intense and dark with need. Lowering his lips to hers, he kissed her with conviction, like if he didn't kiss her now, he would never have the chance again. Their kiss was hot and needy. As he pressed his hips into her, breaching her entrance. The exquisite feel of him filling her, stretching her, was too much, yet not enough. She moved her hips, desperately needing the friction. Pulling back and plunging deeper with each delicious slide, they set a steady rhythm, both giving and taking what they needed from each other. Whitney could feel the sizzle start in her core, and she knew another release was building. The slick heat of Hayden's strong body moving above her was intoxicating, as he rocked into her with long deep strokes that drove her higher with every grind and press of his hips.

He hitched her legs over his shoulders, pressing deeper still, and she ignited. Her inner walls clenching him like a vice, as wave after wave of pleasure took her under. Drowning in the feel of her release, she let out a raspy cry, his body shuddering as he followed her to the crashing waves below.

CHAPTER 7

*H*ayden collapsed to the side, satiated, and spent and pulled Whitney into him. She intertwined her legs with his and they lay there quietly for a moment, catching their breaths, a sheen of sweat covering their naked bodies. Whitney shivered, and Hayden pulled her in tighter. "Are you cold, gorgeous?" She nodded, giving in to another shiver. "Okay, let's get under the covers and I'll warm you up."

Rising from the bed, he pulled back the covers, and she scrambled underneath while he disposed of the condom and joined her under the comforter. "Better?" he asked, nestling her into him, his strong arms around her.

"Yes," she sighed, snuggling into him deeper, her body wrapped around his.

They lay there in silence for a long time and Hayden's mind drifted off into a state of bliss as he reflected on the incredible woman in his arms. Whitney was so much more than he thought she was when they first met. Obviously, she was this stunning, kick ass woman who had the strength to hold her own, but she was also sweet, vulnerable, and guarded. A lot more complex than he had thought. He understood how she may be difficult for some men to understand, but to him, all those qualities she possessed added to her beauty. He loved her layers, and he wanted to continue to peel them back. *Love? Was he falling for Whitney?* Never had that word crept into any other relationship he had. And now it was the first word he thought of when he thought of her.

"What are you thinking?" she asked, lacing her fingers with his as they rested over his chest.

"I was just thinking about how grateful I am," he answered truthfully. "How grateful I am to be here with you. To be able to hold you and how grateful I am that you have chosen to trust me."

She lifted her head, resting her chin on his chest as she reached up to run her fingers through his hair. Meeting his gaze, her lips curved into an affectionate smile.

"Now, knowing more, I know that trust is not easy for you," he continued. "And the fact that you have broken down your walls for me." his voice cracked with unexpected emotion as tears pricked his eyes. "It feels good."

Whitney climbed on top of him, straddling his hips, and ran her hands through his hair. She smoothed her fingertips over his eyebrows and down his face, caressing his cheek affectionately. Running her fingers over his jaw to his lips, she leaned down and tenderly brushed her lips over his. The kiss was so light but electric; it made his heart jolt. Her eyes were dark and shiny, his emotion drawing out her own. Love shone in their depths and even if her head was not ready to acknowledge it yet, it was there, and the feeling was mutual.

"I feel safe with you," she confessed as she kissed him again.

Pulling the covers over them both, he wrapped his powerful arms around her and pulled her into his chest, hugging her and stroking her back lovingly. Knowing what he now knew about Whitney, those words were her *I love you.*

* * *

WHITNEY WOKE THE NEXT MORNING, Hayden spooning her from behind. His taut, naked body enveloping her in tantalizing warmth, and she sighed contentedly. Last night had been, in one word, magical. Their bodies fitting together so seamlessly. They had discovered it was not just sex that drew them together, their connection beyond the physical. There was something intangible between them now, something raw and emotional. Whitney was done fighting their palpable chemistry.

Stirring behind her, Hayden's large hand splayed on her stomach, the heat of it making her core instinctively pulse.

"Good morning," he whispered in her ear. His breath tickling the sensitive skin on her neck. "Did you sleep well?"

"I did," she responded, wiggling her backside into his groin. She could feel him harden under her movements and she giggled. "Someone else is awake."

Hayden laughed groggily. "Little Hayden is always awake when you're around, gorgeous."

"Little Hayden?" she questioned with another giggle. "I would refer to him as Big Hayden."

"Oh, really?" he asked, flipping her over and pinning her hands over her head. She squirmed with laughter, then moaned as he ground himself on her. "How about I show you more of what Big Hayden can do?" he asked, his mouth curving into a sexy grin.

"Yes, please." she teased back, grinding her hips into his.

He climbed off the bed and grabbed his wallet, pulling out a condom. Sheathing himself, he crawled across the bed, mimicking a jungle cat, growling and snarling as he prowled towards her. She laughed in response, and he gave her a playful grin.

"What shall we do?" he asked, putting his hand to his chin in thought as he sat back on his heels. "How about you show me your yoga skills and flip over putting that perfect ass in the air for me?"

"You're bossy." she remarked as she flipped onto her stomach and curled her knees underneath her body.

"You like it," he teased, smoothing his hand over her back, tracing her spine, his touch leaving goosebumps in its wake. Hayden smoothed his hands over her behind and squeezed, then slipped his fingers between her legs, massaging between her folds. She moaned as he circled the bundle of nerves at her centre and dipped a finger into her molten heat, making her cry out with approval.

"You're so wet for me," he said, his voice low and husky as he gripped her hips and sank into her with one long, deep slide. She gasped in pleasure as he pulled himself all the way out and plunged back in even harder.

"Just like that," she cried out as he drove into her, their feral grunts and moans escaping with every punishing thrust. Slowing down his strokes to draw out their pleasure, his sensual movements were sweet torture, as Whitney got lost in each delicious sensation he was eliciting.

"Whitney, I hope you're close because I don't think I can hold back much longer," he panted out as he sank deep with each grind and press.

She clenched, her inner walls gripping him hard in response, and he groaned as he started to lose control. Pulling her up flush with his body, her back to his front and reached between her legs, he strummed her swollen centre, causing her to follow him. White-hot pleasure ripped through her body and her head fell back on his shoulder as he clung to her, both trembling with their release. Bodies still connected, and their chests heaving in unison, Whitney breathed out.

"Hayden, that was…"

"Incredible." Hayden panted as he leaned down and planted kisses along her neck.

Whitney melted into him, feeling connected mind, body, and soul as the last of her walls crumbled to the ground.

THE STORM HAVING DIED DOWN and the roads already safer with the snow ploughs out, Hayden and Whitney checked out of their room and made the three-block trek down the snowy sidewalks back to the arena parking lot. Climbing into his truck, he turned to her. "Are you hungry?"

"Famished." Whitney replied with a glint of innuendo in her eyes.

He chuckled, then winked at her. "Let's get some breakfast."

Not far from the arena, Hayden turned off the main street into an industrial area and pulled into a parking lot in front of a building that resembled an old warehouse.

"What is this place?" Whitney asked, as she got out of the truck and took in the old brick structure, glancing around at the bustle of people coming in and out of the building.

"This is The Forks. It's where the Red River and Assiniboine River meet, and it's been turned into a tourist place with shops and lots of food vendors. They also have lots of activities you can do here all year long."

Whitney's eyes widened with excitement as Hayden took her hand and led her into the building. Walking through the entrance, it opened into a two-story open space with high beamed ceilings and a glass roof letting in natural light. The smell of foreign spices tickled her senses as they passed rows of food vendors peddling their delicious wares amongst the century old brick alcoves. The bright bold colors of the shop awnings brought a sense of whimsy to the space, enticing you to explore and see what treasures you could find in the cute shops and kiosks. Hayden led her down a hall leading into what looked like a large food court, flagged with every type of food vendor your heart desired.

"My favorite place is just over here, around this corner." he gestured, leading her into yet another hallway and into a third open area. There was a vendor whose sign read "All Day Breakfast and Brunch."

"The food here is the best," Hayden explained as they took their place in line.

Whitney's eyes roamed the simple menu and her stomach growled, making them both laugh. "I'll have whatever you're having." she answered. "Surprise me!"

"Okay, that's easy enough." He replied as their turn came up. "Two breakfast specials, an extra order of hash browns and sausage please, and two black coffees."

As he pulled out his wallet to pay for their breakfasts, Hayden asked Whitney to find them a seat around the corner. Finding an open area with about a half dozen tables that faced the windows overlooking the river, she found a free table and took a seat and admired the view outside. The glistening snow covered everything in a soft blanket of white, and the trees that lined the walkway were sparkling with hoarfrost in the bright morning sunshine. Glancing around the dining space, she marveled at the high ceilings with white fairy lights strung up by the beams, giving it a magical feel against the rustic brick walls. *This place is gorgeous.*

"I hope you're hungry!" Hayden exclaimed as he rounded the corner, holding a tray full of food. The smell of sausage, bacon, eggs, fried potatoes, and hot buttered toast filling her senses.

"Wow, this all looks amazing." She said, taking in the spread laid before them.

"I think we worked up an appetite." he winked, flashing her a coquettish grin.

Whitney smiled back, popping a buttery fried potato into her mouth, and letting out a moan of approval. "Oh my, these are crazy good!"

Hayden nodded in agreement and with questioning eyes, he asked. "Speaking of crazy good, how are you feeling about last night?"

"And this morning." she added, giving him a playful wink between bites.

Hayden chuckled and reached out for her hand, meeting her gaze with seriousness. "Are you okay with this?" he asked, pointing between them. "Am I wrong in thinking we have started something amazing here?"

She offered him a soft smile and squeezed his hand. "We have, Hayden."

Hayden let out a long breath, obviously relieved by her answer, then continued. "So, where do we go from here?" he asked, his eyes intense and hopeful.

"Are you asking me if we're dating now?" she asked, meeting his insistent gaze, and glancing away as if contemplating his question. She smiled, returned her gaze to his, and replied. "Yes."

"So, is it safe to assume you're now my girlfriend?" Hayden continued, seeking clarification.

She cocked her head to the side again and searched his inquiring eyes. Her lips curved into a confirming smile. "Yes, Hayden."

Suddenly Hayden jumped up from his chair, letting

out an echoing whoop and pumping his fist into the air. Everyone at their respective tables looked at them, a mix of confusion and amusement on their faces. Whitney laughed, her face reddening, and shook her head at his very public show. Taking her hand and bringing her to her feet, he swooped her up into a huge hug, lifting her off the ground. A security guard came around the corner, scrutinizing them both.

"Is everything okay over here?" the security guard asked, his hand poised on his radio.

"This beautiful woman just agreed to be my girlfriend!" Hayden bellowed, eliciting snickers and few claps from the other patrons.

The security guard smiled, shook his head, and let out a little chuckle. "As you were, then," he said, gesturing to them both.

Whitney laughed and met Hayden's twinkling eyes. His sweet and unexpected reaction made her heart burst with happiness. Hayden had proven to her he was trustworthy and would never intentionally hurt her. He was like no other man she had ever met, and after everything she had been through in the past, she needed some goodness in her life. Hayden represented a second chance, and she deserved to see where this relationship would take them.

A FEW DAYS LATER, Ben and Ever returned from their honeymoon. Hayden and Whitney, eager to see them and share their news, made plans to meet them at the Eazy for lunch.

Hayden noticed Ben's truck was already in the lot and let out a long exhale.

"Are you nervous, Hayden?" Whitney asked, putting her hand on his thigh.

"A little," he admitted, parking next to Ben's truck. "Not sure why, though. I mean, this is my brother and Ever is one of your closest friends. It's just, Ben has always been critical of my dating life, and I just want them to approve of us."

Whitney leaned over and kissed him softly in reassurance. "It'll be fine. Trust me."

Getting out of his truck, Hayden took her hand, and they entered the building together. Immediately Ever spotted them, waving from a table in the middle of the café. Both Ever and Ben got up and hugged them. Whitney beamed, overjoyed to see her friend, who looked tanned and glowing from her tropical vacation. Hayden pulled out Whitney's chair, as she sat down across from Ever and Hayden across from Ben.

"You two look amazing! How was Hawaii?" Hayden asked.

Ever looked at Ben, who smiled lovingly at her. "It was heavenly," she shared. "The weather, the water, the people, the food! Oh my goodness the food. I could live on pineapple the rest of my life and die happy."

Ben laughed his big, booming laugh. "It was really beautiful," he added simply in his deep baritone.

"Well, I for one, can't wait to see the pictures." Whitney

added, taking Hayden's hand under the table, sensing his continued apprehension.

They all smiled from one to the other as an atypical awkwardness fell over their group. Whitney surveyed Ever, her eyes dancing and over to Ben, with a subtle smile tugging at his lips.

"I feel like you two have something to tell us," Whitney observed, cocking her head to the side.

Ever looked at Ben and he nodded, as if giving her the okay to share. "I'm pregnant." Ever replied, her eyes exuding pure joy and happiness.

Whitney's eyes widened and Hayden reached over, slapping his brother on his shoulder. "You waste no time, Brother!" Hayden teased.

Ben flashed Hayden his signature scowl, which softened into a warm smile as he took in Ever's unbridled excitement.

"Honestly, I had a suspicion at the wedding but had been feeling good. No serious morning sickness. So, when we got to the island, I bought a test, and well, it came back positive."

Whitney rose from her seat, Ever following suit, and the women hugged. "I'm so incredibly happy for you both."

"I have an appointment in two weeks, along with an ultrasound to make sure things are okay." Ever continued.

"That is so exciting!" Whitney replied, delight in her tone as she and Ever returned to their seats. "So, we have a little something to share with you two as well." Whitney started as she laced her fingers with Hayden's under the table.

"Are you pregnant too?" Ever asked, a teasing smile on her lips.

Whitney gave her friend a roll of her eyes and she glanced back at Hayden who was now smiling wide, his grin ear to ear. *I'm going to have to revisit that later.*

"No." she laughed as she held up their intertwined hands. "But we are a couple."

Ever looked from Hayden to Whitney and back to Hayden, an approving smile covering her face. Ben leaned back in his chair with amusement and folded his arms over his broad chest.

"You two are…" Ever trailed off.

"We are dating." Hayden finished her sentence.

Ever squealed excitedly, causing a table full of local farmers to turn their heads at the sound. "Sorry." she apologized as she turned her attention back to Whitney and Hayden.

"So, when did this happen?" Ben asked, showing genuine interest, but still looking stoic at their news.

"Well, officially this past weekend." Hayden continued. "I know it's not as big as having a baby, but we're happy."

Ever shook her head. "It's very good news, Hayden. Ben and I are super happy for you, aren't we, Ben?" she commented, giving Ben a chiding glare to acknowledge their news.

"Yes! Very good." Ben added, then smiled back at Ever for her approval.

"And Whitney, you're officially moving here?" Ever continued. "I know this is going to be a big change for you."

"It is." Whitney agreed. "But I think it'll be a good one,"

she added as she snuggled closer to Hayden, and he put his arm around her. "Hayden has already made me feel very at home here. I've had the opportunity to meet with a few of the local artists I will be working with, and since my work can be done remotely, I'm not exactly sure what I'll be doing yet, but I may open my own agency here in Manitoba."

Ever's eyes widened. "That would be amazing!"

"I think so too." Whitney agreed.

"Wow, I feel like so much has happened in the past two weeks since we've been away!" Ever commented, sitting back in her seat. "I'm so happy you're here Whitney and this…" she gestured between Hayden and Whitney, "is simply wonderful!"

CHAPTER 8

Whitney and Hayden continued in domestic bliss. Although nothing was formally discussed, Hayden had moved himself back into the main bedroom with her. Spending their nights making love, they would find themselves falling asleep in each other's arms. With them both in a happy state of cohabitation, Whitney's permanent living arrangements were put on hold, neither discussing nor making a definite decision. They simply carried on, trying not to overthink their new relationship.

Whitney entered Hastings Hardware to pick up Hayden after his workday. Her day taking longer than usual, Hayden said she would be able to find him in the storage room working on a project. A handsome, dark-haired teenage boy with thick, dark-rimmed glasses greeted her with a smile.

"Hi, there! How can I help you?"

Whitney smiled at him kindly. "Hi! I'm Hayden's girl-friend, Whitney. Hayden said he would be in the back."

"Yes, just go through the employee door over there," the teen offered, gesturing straight ahead.

"Thank-you. And your name is?"

"Oh, I am Ryker Hastings." he replied with a sweet smile. "I'm Ben and Hayden's cousin."

"Yes, that's right! I remember meeting you and your family at the wedding."

"Yes, ma'am."

"Just through that door?" she asked, gesturing to the door at the end of the aisle marked Employees Only.

"Yes." Ryker confirmed as he went back around the counter.

Whitney strode off to the back, the click of her high heel boots sounding on the linoleum floor. Pushing through the door, she spotted Hayden past the shelves of stock. Not wanting to startle him, she crept forward quietly. Glancing around, she marvelled at the impressive workshop occupying a large space at the back of the storeroom. There was a long worktable spanned the length of the space and along the wall behind him were a variety of tools organized and hung on a huge peg wall. Underneath the peg wall, shelves held other power tools and bins of wood scraps. On another wall longer lengths of wood rested, waiting to be used for future projects, and a band saw occupied the opposite wall. There was sawdust on the floor and on the worktable. Hayden sat on a stool at the table, safety glasses on, creating a pattern in a long piece of wood with a scroll saw.

Whitney leaned against a shelf and crossed her legs, enjoying the view of him working. So focused on his project, he didn't notice her standing there watching him.

She admired how sexy he looked in a blue and green flannel work shirt rolled up to the elbows showing off his muscular forearms, low slung faded jeans, and brown leather tool belt. His hair was perfectly mussed, as if he had run his hands through it many times, and she bit her bottom lip, thinking about running her hands through it too. Perhaps giving it a playful little tug to make him groan. Whitney continued to watch him and once he put down the saw, she cleared her throat. He met her gaze, and a warm welcoming smile curved his lips.

"How long have you been standing there?" he asked, taking off his safety glasses and setting them on the worktable.

Whitney looked at her watch and gave him a coy grin. "I don't know, about five minutes or so."

Hayden laughed, the sound low and deep, as Whitney sauntered around the worktable, adding a little extra sway to her hips, while he followed each alluring move. Reaching him, she turned, leaning her body seductively against the table, his eyes trained on hers.

Moving his project over to the side, he rose from the stool, removed his leather tool belt, and swiped his hand across the bench, letting the sawdust and pieces of wood fall to the floor.

With a quickening pulse, Whitney licked her lips and gazed up at him through her long lashes.

"Don't look at me like that," he warned, as he lifted her onto the workbench and nestled his body between her legs.

"Like what?" she teased, swiping the tip of her tongue over her lips, knowing he would notice.

"Like you want me to take you, right here on my worktable," he answered, sliding his hands under her skirt, up her thighs, and gripping her hips, and pulling her closer. His body was hard and powerful towering over her and making her ridiculously aroused.

"Maybe I do," she answered, leaning back on her palms, cocking her head to the side, and flashing him a mischievous grin.

"You know Ryker could walk in here anytime."

"I know." she replied, never leaving his gaze as she sat up and reached for the button of his jeans.

Hayden's blue eyes darkened with desire as he slid his hand around the back of her head, tangling in her hair and crashed his lips to hers in a scorching kiss.

Whitney ran her hands under his flannel shirt to feel his warm, ripped chest and stomach, then around to his broad, robust back, feeling the ripple of his muscles under her fingertips. The sheer feel of his strength making her pool with need. Sliding her fingers under the waist of his jeans, she slid her hands inside and squeezed his taut behind, causing him to release her lips and throw his head back in a husky, guttural groan.

"Whitney, you're playing with fire," he warned.

"Then burn me," she replied, her voice raw and wanton as she slid down the zipper of his jeans and reached inside to grip his hard length with her palm.

Hayden's eyes blazed with heat at her touch. Without any further pretense, he pulled out his wallet, retrieved a condom and made quick work sheathing himself. Laying her back on the table, he lifted her skirt till it bunched at her waist, pulled her panties to the side, and feeling her wet and ready for him, he took her, hard and deep with a single thrust. Whitney cried out, her body accepting all of him as he let out a groan of appreciation while he drove into her again and again. The echoes of their moans and skin connecting filling the large room and Whitney could feel her release build fast and furious as he grabbed her hips and pounded into her. With one more punishing thrust, her climax crested and she let out a long-drawn-out moan that seemed to come from a place unworldly. Hayden continued unrelenting until his own release came and he collapsed on top of her. Both lay there a moment, still connected, half dressed and disheveled, as post coital tremors surged through their bodies. Whitney sifted her fingers through his soft hair as they came down from the high.

Just then, the door opened on the other side of the storeroom and their eyes met in surprise. Whitney's eyes widened, and Hayden lifted his head, knowing they couldn't be seen from the door.

"Hayden, do you know if we sell S hooks?" Ryker shouted in question.

"Yes, aisle four near the command hooks."

"Okay, thanks!"

The storeroom door clicked shut and Hayden, still on top of her, flashed Whitney an amused smile, causing her to giggle. Rising off the table, he discarded the condom and straightened himself out, helping lift Whitney from the worktable as she rolled her skirt back down.

"Well, that was fun," Whitney commented, smoothing out her skirt and dusting the wood shavings off the fabric, as Hayden removed a little piece of wood from her hair.

"Agreed." he replied, flashing her a sexy grin as he pulled her into him and wrapped his arms around her giving her a hug.

Releasing his embrace, Whitney took in his workspace again, the project he was working on capturing her attention. She picked it up and inspected it curiously, then glanced up at him as if to ask, *what is this?*

"I'm working on a crib for Ben and Ever." he shared.

Whitney's eyes brightened, and she looked back at the piece in her hands.

"I've made some furniture before, but this will be the first crib I've built."

Offering him a smile, she ran her fingers over the intricate carving he had completed so far. "You are so talented, Hayden." she complimented as she marveled at the details. He had put into what she guessed was going to be the headboard of the crib.

"Thanks." he smiled proudly. "I want to carve the headboard with farm animals as it could fit either a boy or a girl."

"That is so sweet, Hayden." she whispered, an unexpected lump of emotion catching in her throat.

"If their crib turns out like I hope, maybe someday I'll make one for my child," he shared, taking the piece of wood from her hands and smoothing his hand over it.

Whitney glanced up at him, and she could see the longing in his eyes. "You want kids?" she asked, searching his gaze.

"I do, someday. A house full, God willing."

She smiled and her heart aching from his sweet declaration. She had always dreamt of having a family. A sweet little chubby faced baby with ten little fingers and ten little toes. She could almost smell the sweet baby powder as a deep pang of longing bore its way into her chest. An ache she felt so many times before. That deep, indescribable yearning for a child of her own. Just then a flashback clouded her thoughts, and Paul's unkind words pierced into her.

Are you an idiot? Did you think I would fall for that trick? From now on I want to see you take your pills every day! My wife is not going to get fat and disgusting!

She shivered and shook her head as if that could wipe the memory from her consciousness.

"Where did you go just now?" Hayden asked, his brows furrowed with concern as he put his hands on her hips and pulled her in close to him.

Whitney turned away, breaking eye contact, not wanting Hayden to see the deep, painful emotion that was breaching the surface. Swallowing down hard, her throat ached as tears threatened to escape.

Hayden turned her head back to face him and lifted her chin to meet his worried eyes as he whispered, "You can tell me."

She let out a long breath to steady her mounting emotion as she replied. "I was just thinking about how my ex didn't want to have kids. He always accused me of not taking my birth control and trying to get pregnant behind his back. He'd get so mad, screaming at me that he didn't want me to get pregnant as no wife of his was going to be fat and disgusting."

Hayden's eyes blazed with anger, and he stared at her, frustration covering his face. After a moment he took her face into his hands, his eyes intense as he replied. "Whitney, you're going to be so beautiful pregnant." he said lovingly, so much conviction in his tone. "And you're going to be the most amazing mother."

This man. She stared into this handsome face, tears spilling down her cheeks. She blinked, her tears hot and searing, the pain of the past burning her skin.

"Don't cry, Whitney." he cooed softly as he ran his palms over her wet cheeks and leaned down, brushing his lips over hers in an excruciatingly tender kiss. As he kissed her with tenderness, sincerity, and reassurance, she realized, right then, with every part of her being, that she was madly, irrevocably, without question, in love with Hayden Hastings.

HAYDEN AND WHITNEY walked up to Ben and Ever's farmhouse, a pie plate in hand. They had been invited for dinner and Whitney was eager to talk with Ever about her recent doctor's appointment.

Ever opened the door even before they could knock. "You're here!" she exclaimed, hugging them both and inviting them in. Ben stood at the front entrance, his blue eyes crackling with excitement.

"Ben, you look like the cat that swallowed the canary." Hayden commented with amusement at his brother's atypical expression.

Rather than giving his brother his usual growl and scowl, Ben laughed and welcomed them into the living room. A fire was lit in the stone fireplace and the flicker of the flames made light dance on the walls. It made the entire room inviting, warm and cozy. Taking a seat at one end of the long leather couch, Hayden pulled Whitney in next to him, his arm snuggly around her waist. Ben took a seat at the other side and Ever nestled into his lap, as they often did. Both glanced at each other, their smiles growing even wider.

"Okay, spill!" Whitney ordered. "I want to know what the doctor said!"

Ben turned to Ever, and she nodded for him to share their news.

"Ever and I found out yesterday we're having twins." Ben shared excitedly, as he ran his hand over Ever's belly, the evidence of her baby bump already showing.

Hayden and Whitney's eyes widened in surprise. "Wow, you guys, that's incredible!" Hayden congratulated. "Two babies!"

Ever nodded, her face beaming with unbridled joy as Whitney, tears forming in her eyes, reached out to Ever. The friends wrapped their arms around each other, both letting the tears of happiness fall. Hayden leaned over and put out his fist to bump Ben's. He had never seen his brother happier and more excited about anything in his life. Seeing his brother find such joy and contentment stirred both feelings of envy and hope within him. Hayden was self admittedly jealous that Ben had found what he so deeply desired for himself, but it also gave him hope that he would have that too.

His eyes locked on Whitney who was wiping the tears from her face, and she turned to capture his gaze, smiling at him sweetly. *Could I have it all with Whitney?* Reflecting on their conversation in his workshop, he knew she wanted the life Ben and Ever had found too. She wanted her person, a happy marriage and she wanted a family. *But did she want that with me?* With his insecurities rearing their ugly head and making him question everything, he shook his head, trying to dispel the negative thoughts. He loved Whitney. If he was being completely honest with himself, he had been in love with her from the night they met. And as they spent more time together, getting to know each other better, it only solidified his initial feelings for her. He was in love with Whitney Faris. Now to show her he was the man for her.

* * *

AFTER DINNER AND A LONG VISIT, Hayden helped Whitney into his truck and leaned in to give her a chaste kiss. "I want to take you somewhere," he said, giving her a wink.

"Now? It's late," she questioned, her eyes glinting with curiosity.

"Yes, I promise you're going to love it!"

Hayden hopped into the cab and started down the long driveway, turning onto the gravel road, the opposite direction from his place. Whitney stared out the window at the snow-covered ditches lighting their way as he navigated down the dark road. Two miles from Prairie Sky, he pulled onto a utility road, driving over low snowbanks, and making a path through the snow. They stopped, enrobed in darkness, with fields surrounding them on either side.

"Where are we?" she asked curiously, glancing out at

the darkness, just the moonlight on the snow providing a faint ethereal glow.

Hayden smiled and turned to her. "Trust me?" he asked, as he turned off the engine and the headlights of the truck, enveloping them in the cover of night.

"Yes, I trust you," she answered with some hesitation in her voice.

He opened his door and reached for her as she shimmied to the driver's side. Helping her out of the cab, he grabbed their mittens that were in the middle console of the truck. Handing her the mittens, she put them on and hooked her arm into his.

"Watch your step," he cautioned as he guided her towards the back of the truck and unlatched the tailgate. He lifted her onto the tailgate and climbed up next to her. Taking his hand in hers, he leaned into her, his warm breath at her ear. "Look up," he whispered.

Whitney's eyes rose to the sky and the most glorious blanket of stars greeted her. There were millions, shining brightly and sparkling like glitter against the obsidian sky.

"It's amazing!" she whispered; her voice was full of wonder.

The prairie night was like a dream, more brilliant than she could have imagined. So, unlike the faint glint of stars she would see, between the flood of city lights back in Toronto. This was a pure unobstructed view of God's wonder. Just then, a bright light streak across the sky. A shooting star.

"Did you see that?" She asked Hayden, as he wrapped his arm around Whitney to keep her warm.

"I did," he replied. "Did you make a wish?"

"I did," she answered, resting her head contentedly on his shoulder.

"What did you wish for?"

"I can't tell you!" she giggled as she squeezed his arm. "Then it won't come true."

"I am not sure I believe that," he confessed, kissing the top of her head. "My wish has already come true."

Whitney glanced up at him, barely making out her features in the dark.

"I wished for someone like you. I love you, Whitney." he professed, not wanting to hold back his feelings anymore. Hearing her breath hitch with his declaration, she exhaled, the smoky tendrils of her warm breath swirling around her in the cold winter night. Whitney's hand came up, cupping his cheek, her thumb smoothing over it affectionately.

"I love you too, Hayden." she whispered on a breath, her words the sweetest sound to his ear. Pulling him closer, their hot breaths mingling as Whitney found his lips in the dark and kissed him long and deep, as all doubts as to her feelings for him dissipated.

Breaking their embrace, Hayden hopped down from the tailgate, spread his arms out wide and yelled towards the night sky. "Whitney Faris loves me!"

Whitney laughed at his proclamation to the universe as he stalked over and captured his lips in another passionate kiss. Their love, like two radiant stars lighting up the prairie night.

CHAPTER 9

Hayden pulled into the drive of Prairie Sky and made his way to the barn. It was late afternoon on a Saturday, and Ben needed help to prepare the barn for the winter months. The late November cold had fully set in, along with copious amounts of snow, so they needed to prepare space for the animals.

"Hey, Bro." Hayden greeted his brother, who was getting some feed into a pail to help them wrangle up the livestock.

"Hayden, glad you're here," he responded, handing him a pail of feed. "Ever would have helped me with this, but I want her to take it easy over the next while."

"You realize, Ever, Whitney and Bea are out shopping right now in St. Augustine, right?" Hayden asked.

"Yeah, I know, but I just don't want her hurting herself in the barn or with the livestock."

Hayden nodded and gave his brother a grin, knowing how protective he was with Ever. Now, with two babies on the way, his protective instincts were tenfold.

As they bedded the box stalls with straw, Hayden glanced at his big brother and asked. "Are you ready to be a dad?"

Ben met his gaze with a broad, happy smile covering his face. "As ready as I'll ever be."

Hayden looked at his brother, imagining this larger-than-life man holding two little bundles in his arms. His heart swelled with joy at the thought as he commented. "You are going to be an awesome dad!"

Ben, a man of few words, grinned his simple way of thanking him for the compliment. "So, how are things going with you and Whitney?" he asked, turning the tables.

"Great! After dinner here last weekend, I brought her out to Baker's field."

Ben stopped what he was doing, his eyes darting over to Hayden, a smile tugging at his lips. "Did you bring her there to show her the stars?" Ben asked, that spot well known as a sort of lover's lane in Primrose.

"I did, and to tell her I love her," he replied, bracing himself for Ben's reaction.

"What did she say?" Ben asked, squinting his eyes.

"She said she loves me, too."

Ben flashed him an approving smile. "Hayden, I'm truly happy for you."

Hayden felt emotion rise in his chest at his brother's approval. Having looked up to big brother his entire life, his support meant the world to him. Simply knowing that his brother acknowledged his happiness and approved of his relationship with Whitney was all he needed.

* * *

WHITNEY, Ever and Bea settled into a table in the corner of a gourmet coffee shop in St. Augustine.

"I miss coffee already." Ever lamented, staring sadly at her cup of rooibos tea.

"Poor babies." Bea remarked, reaching over to touch Ever's belly.

Whitney laughed at Bea's response and took a sip of her black coffee, savoring the warm, bitter liquid.

"So, the Primrose rumour mill is going crazy," mentioned Bea with a look of inquiry on her face. "Lots of buzz about a certain handsome hardware store owner and his fancy city girlfriend."

"Really!" Whitney laughed.

"You know you're part of the community when you're being gossiped about," Bea said with a wink as she stirred her latte. "So, catch me up!" Bea exclaimed, sitting back and crossing her arms over her chest. "I feel a little out of the loop."

"Do you want the nutshell version?" Whitney asked, her eyebrows raised in question.

"Sure!" Ever replied, leaning towards her, curiosity in her eyes.

"After our first date, Hayden and I revisited our initial connection." She shared, wiggling her eyebrows and making both Bea and Ever giggle. "After that, we officially started dating and last weekend I told him I loved him." She confessed as she quickly took another sip of her coffee and waited for her friends' reactions.

"You what?" Ever asked, eyes widening. "You love

him?"

Whitney nodded and grinned brightly at her friends, knowing how significant it was that she had just dropped the "L" bomb. "I love Hayden very much." She confirmed with deep sincerity as she looked at her friends. "I don't think I've ever felt this strong about anyone before."

Bea sat back, let out a huge huff of breath and laughed. "Well, gosh darn it! I have missed a lot! And this all happened in the past two weeks?"

Whitney nodded, a radiant smile on her face.

"Wow!" Bea exclaimed. "I'm so glad your feelings finally caught up with him."

"What do you mean?" Whitney asked, confused, and leaning in closer with curiosity.

"She means Hayden has been in love with you since you met," Ever added, taking a sip of her tea. "I'm pretty sure for Hayden; it was love at first sight."

Whitney sat back and blinked; not sure she believed what they were telling her.

Bea nodded her head in agreement with Ever. "You must understand something about Hayden. The guy is a hopeless romantic. He has never been afraid of love or sharing his life with someone. And he has been wanting a committed relationship for a long time." Bea added. "The problem was he was meeting all the wrong kinds of girls. Women who are superficial and not worthy of his kindness or selflessness. He's been taken advantage of so many times. Just women seeing what's on the surface, but no one really taking the time to get to know the truly amazing guy he is in here." Bea pointed to her heart.

"Ben has told me stories." Ever commented, shaking her head.

Bea went on, "Seriously, Hayden has wanted someone to share his life with for a long time. Even with all his attempts at something more meaningful, he never gave up and was always optimistic, even when he got hurt in the process. And Whitney, he got hurt a lot."

Whitney stared at Bea unblinking, her words about Hayden going straight to her heart. She had let her first impression of him shadow her judgement in the beginning and now, having gotten to know more about Hayden; he had met and surpassed her expectations. He wanted something meaningful and true, and he wanted it with her. Whitney smiled thoughtfully into her coffee cup.

"I assume he told you he loves you too?" Ever asked.

"He did." Whitney replied. "Honestly, meeting Hayden took me completely by surprise. You know, Ever, I wasn't really looking for anyone."

"I know." Ever nodded. "Does he know your history, with your past relationship?"

"He knows everything."

Ever and Bea gave her approving nods, knowing how significant it was for Whitney to share her entire past with Hayden. Whitney reached out and took the hands of her friends, giving them a squeeze, overwhelmed by the support her friends were giving her new relationship. Never had she ever thought that she would be head over heels in love with a small-town boy from Manitoba and want more than anything to build a life with him.

* * *

DECEMBER CAME to Primrose bringing more snow and turning the small town into a Winter Wonderland. Hayden, determined to give Whitney the full country Christmas experience, brought her to a local tree farm so they could pick out a tree together.

"How do you know which tree to pick?" Whitney asked as they made their way through the rows of trees.

"No real method to it." Hayden laughed, holding an axe in his hand. "Just pick one you think looks good."

Whitney stopped and inspected a few trees, touching the needles and smelling them. Taking her in, he smiled at how impossibly cute she was travelling from tree to tree, this experience something new and exciting for her.

The past five weeks with Whitney had been wonderful and she fully emersed herself in small town life. Although there was so much more to discover about her, each day as they grew closer, the illusive sense of completeness he had desired for so long was becoming a reality. The completeness his mother talked about when she shared about his father. That feeling that you are with the person made just for you and the more time he spent with Whitney he was sure she was the one.

"This tree looks nice!" Whitney exclaimed, looking up at a huge Douglas Fir.

"Nice pick," he complimented as he knelt and positioned himself to cut down the tree.

Whitney stood back and watched with curiosity as he swung the axe at the trunk of the tree. With only a handful of swings, the tree was down, and Hayden stood up straight, a look of accomplishment on his face.

Whitney's eyes flashed at him. "Is it weird that I found that very sexy?" She confessed with a coquettish grin.

"Lumberjack porn," he elaborated, flexing his muscles with the axe in hand.

Whitney laughed, reached down, and scooped up some snow, forming it into a ball. A snowball smashed into Hayden's chest. Surprised, he glanced at Whitney, and she let out a playful giggle.

Cocking an eyebrow at her, Hayden dropped his ax next to the fallen tree. Reaching down, he grabbed a handful of snow and stalked over to her. Not knowing exactly what he was going to do, she turned, ready to bolt down the path. He caught her by the waist, and she squealed, her giggle echoing in the crisp, open air. Holding out the fist full of snow in front of her face, ready to wash her with it, but he paused, unsure of how she may react if he did it.

"Don't you dare!" she chided in warning.

Listening, he released her and dropped the snow in his hand, then turned back to their fallen tree. With his back turned, Whitney quickly scooped another handful and reached around him, giving him a face full of snow. Hayden sputtered and wiped his face with his gloved hands, then turned to her, his eyes twinkling as he let out a wicked laugh. She flashed him a teasing, "come and get me" look in return.

"Now you've asked for it!" he said as he grabbed another handful of snow and before she could get away, he hooked her around the waist, this time rubbing the snow into her face. She turned to face him, her face red and wet from the cold ambush. His eyebrows knit together as he surveyed her, waiting for her reaction to his retaliating snow wash. Whitney wiped at her face as her lips curved into a smile. Letting out a relieved breath, he put out his arms to hug her, but she ran at him, knocking him down into the snow. Startled, he started to laugh as she straddled his hips and smiled down at him with another handful of snow poised over his face.

"Surrender!" she commanded, a determined and mischievous look on her face.

"I surrender," he replied, putting his hands up in the air.

She laughed, dropping the snow and taunted with a giggle. "I win."

"You win," he echoed, gripping the back of her neck to pull her closer for a passionate kiss. Pulling back from his embrace, Whitney fell to the side next to him in the snow. Hayden turned his head to face the woman he loved, pure joy twinkling in her eyes. Everything about her radiated beauty, and he was in awe. Her face flushed with the cold, ice kissing her long lashes and rosy lips curved into a sweet smile. *How did I get so lucky?*

HAYDEN AND WHITNEY sat on the couch, admiring their handiwork. The fully decorated tree stood before them, beautiful lights twinkling, garland strung, and ornaments hung.

"I love all your handmade ornaments." she commented, nestling into his warm chest.

"My Mom made most of them," he commented. "She always loved to do crafts and always had DIY projects going."

"Can you tell me about her?" Whitney asked, meeting his gaze.

Hayden smiled, nostalgia washing over his face as he reflected on his mother. "My mom was kind and always helping others when they needed help. She always put her family first and was very selfless. She had the best laugh, one of those laughs that made you turn your head, like you wanted to know where it came from. She was the best cook; she could literally make anything. She always gave the best advice and encouraged us to be whatever we wanted to be. I adored her."

"She sounds amazing." Whitney commented, her eyes trained on Hayden.

"She was. She and I were super close."

"You must miss her."

"I do, every day," he answered. "I wish she could have met you. You two would have been thick as thieves."

"I would have loved to have met her, too." Whitney confessed. "What was the best advice she ever gave you?"

"To love big," he said. "She would always say, Hayden, when you find the one for you, love big. Hold on and never let go."

Silence fell over them both as they reflected on those words and watched the lights sparkle on the tree. Breaking their reverie, Hayden spoke. "Whitney, I know you had no intention of staying here with me forever in this house. But I can't imagine not having you here every day," he confessed. "Will you move in with me, officially that is?" Whitney turned her head, meeting his gaze. "I know we haven't been dating long, but I know I love you and want to see where this goes. Plus, you need a place to live. I want you to live here with me."

Whitney peeled herself from him, rose from the couch and climbed onto his lap, straddling his hips. She cupped his cheek and ran her thumb over his bottom lip affectionately, meeting his eyes as she answered, "Hayden, yes, I will move in here, officially." She smiled and brushed her lips over his.

"But there is one more very important thing we need to do, to seal this living arrangement agreement," he said, a serious look on his face.

"What's that?"

He waggled his eyebrows playfully, his eyes darting towards the hallway leading to their bedroom. Whitney gave him a seductive smile, climbed off him and put out her hand to help him up. He smiled up at her and took her hand rising from the couch. Leaning in, he kissed her softly, then in one big swoop, hoisted her over his shoulder, making her squeal.

"Big man has big love to give his woman!" he exclaimed in an attempted caveman voice as he carried down the hall to their bedroom.

WHITNEY DIALED her parent's number in Arizona, waiting for the video to connect. "Hi Mom! Hi Dad!"

"Whitney, sweetheart!" her mother cooed. "We haven't seen you in so long!"

"I know. Sorry about that. I've been going through some big changes recently."

Both of her parents leaned closer to the screen, a mix of concern and curiosity on their faces.

Obliging their curiosity, Whitney continued. "Rosenburg Agencies closed, as Ned decided to retire and passed all his Manitoba artists to me."

"Is that where you are now, then?" her mother questioned.

"Yes, I've actually decided to move here."

"Oh, my goodness, that is a big change," her mother pointed out. "You've always lived in Toronto."

"It's definitely different, but I love it here." Whitney smiled, reflecting on her new small-town life. "I am living near Primrose, so I'm close to Ever and Ben."

"Oh, how is that sweet girl doing?" her mother asked.

Ever, not having family in Toronto, had spent many a holiday with the Faris family, Whitney's parents treating her like another daughter.

"She's wonderful! She's expecting twins in spring!"

Both of her parents beamed, and her mother clapped her hands with excitement.

"Please give her our well wishes." her father replied.

"I will, Dad."

"Now, Whitney, I can see you have something to share with us," her mother coaxed. "A mother can tell these things."

Whitney laughed and nervously cleared her throat, hearing Hayden shuffle beside her and take a seat on the stool. "I've met someone, and he's become really special to me."

Her mother's eyes widened, and a huge smile enveloped her face. "You have? That's wonderful! Tell me about him."

"His name is Hayden Hastings. He's Ben's brother, and he's here with me, right now, if you want to meet him." she replied nervously, turning to Hayden and adjusting her laptop to bring Hayden onto the screen.

"Hello, Mr. and Mrs. Faris, it's a pleasure to meet you!" Hayden greeted, with a smile and a little wave.

Whitney's mother grinned with approval, and Whitney's father squinted, giving Hayden a scrutinizing look.

"Oh, please call us Dan and Betty!" her mother insisted.

"Okay, then." Hayden agreed, moving himself closer to Whitney.

Whitney's father folded his arms, obviously sizing Hayden up. "What is it you do, Hayden?"

"I own a local hardware store, and, on the side, I do custom woodworking." Whitney's father nodded, a small smile tugging at his lips. "The hardware store was my parents' store until they passed away, so I took over the family business about four years ago."

Betty gave him a sympathetic look. "You must miss them this time of year."

"I do very much, but I have my brother, Ever and now Whitney." he smiled, putting his arm around her affectionately.

Whitney looked at him, meeting his gaze. His ease brought her comfort. "I wanted to call, Mom and Dad, as I won't be able to come to Arizona for Christmas this year. With all the changes, I need to stay here." Whitney shared.

"And you want to spend Christmas with Hayden?" Her mother added with a wink. Whitney nodded. "Oh, honey, enjoy your Christmas together. The first Christmas is an exciting time. And don't worry about us, your brother and his family are coming out and I'm honestly just happy you're not alone for the holidays."

"Thank you for understanding." Whitney replied, taking Hayden's hand in hers. "I'm looking forward to my first Christmas in the country."

They continued their video chat and Whitney could see her parent's shoulders ease as they talked openly with Hayden. He was a natural charmer, and before the call ended it was obvious her mother was already smitten. Her father was a harder sell, but once they started talking about his love of hockey and how their first date was to an NHL game, her father warmed up to Hayden, too.

With every moment and every first step they took as a couple, Hayden always met and surpassed every expectation. He just kept the surprises coming.

CHAPTER 10

Hayden spent every spare moment he had in his workshop completing a Christmas gift he was making for Whitney. He picked out a chisel and started to carve, making precise grooves into the wood. He smiled, taking in his craftsmanship and hoping Whitney would like it. He wanted nothing more than their first Christmas together to be special and memorable. And with this personal gift he had designed for her, he wanted it to be something she cherished for years to come.

He heard the door to the back room opened, and he quickly put the piece he was carving on the shelf under his worktable, not wanting Whitney to see it.

"Hey there Hay Bale!" Bea exclaimed, her red hair a blaze coming into view.

Hayden shook his head at her nickname for him and flashed her a welcoming smile. Having known Bea for pretty much his entire life, he was used to her nicknames and teasing. Their relationship was like an annoying little sister, even though Bea was older than him. Despite their dynamic, he appreciated her. She was a kind, loyal and thoughtful and always had his best interest at heart. Plus, she wasn't afraid to voice her opinions or give him advice. She was without question one of his closest friends.

"Hey, there Bee-sting!" he volleyed, pinching her arm.

She smacked him hard on the back. How so much force came from her tiny body, always marveled at him.

"What brings you to me ole workshop?" he asked, attempting a British accent.

Bea laughed, appreciating his attempt and giving him a thumbs up. "I was just picking up some Christmas lights and Ryker said you were in the back," she replied, browsing around his workshop, picking up pieces he was working on and inspecting them. "What are these?" she asked, pointing to the carved headboards leaning against the wall.

"Those are the headboards for the cribs I'm making for Ben and Ever's twins," he replied proudly, reaching out to smooth his hand over his carvings.

"Look at you! The favorite uncle, already." she commented, meeting his eyes. "Seriously, though, these are beautiful!" she appraised, running her hands over the hand carved design.

"Thanks, they're coming together nicely."

She continued her perusal of his workspace and her eyes zoning in on his gift for Whitney under his work-table. "What is that?" she asked, reaching for it.

Hayden swooped in before her and placed it down on the tabletop.

Bea inspected his handiwork closely, and she smiled

brightly. "Hayden, this is gorgeous." She complimented, taking in the intricate carvings.

"It's Whitney's Christmas gift," he shared proudly, admiring all the work he was putting into this project.

Bea looked up at him, a huge smile on her face, her green eyes dancing with delight. "You really love her, don't you?" she asked.

Hayden nodded, offering her a resolute smile, "Whitney's the one, Bea."

Although he had always been open with Bea about his love life and he knew she was not one to mince words when she had an opinion. If Bea thought he was rushing things, she was going to call him out on it. He put his hands in his pockets and rocked back and forth in his work boots, waiting for her response.

Bea's lips curved into a kind smile, and she curled her arm around his waist in a half hug. "I am truly happy for you, Hayden."

Hayden could feel the breath he was holding, slowly releasing.

Bea laughed, giving him a punch in the arm and rolled her green eyes at him. "Are you going to Prairie Sky on Christmas Eve?" she asked, as she slung her purse over her shoulder.

"We'll be there," he replied.

She smiled and turned on her heel, giving him a quick glance over her shoulder. "It's nice to see you happy, Hayden. It's about time."

THE CHRISTMAS SEASON had arrived in Primrose, and the excitement of the holidays in a small town was something Whitney had never experienced. Part of what made it so special was the people. They genuinely wanted to make her feel welcome and part of their community, inviting and including her in the festivities. Whitney felt like she belonged here, confirming to her she had made the right decision to move to Primrose.

On Christmas Eve they all attended the church service in town and then gathered at Prairie Sky afterwards for appetizers, drinks, and general holiday merriment.

"How are you doing, Mama?" Whitney asked, putting her hand on Ever's now very noticeable belly. Four months along, Ever seemed to have popped overnight.

"Good," she replied, giving her a tired smile. "Not sleeping well, though. I started to feel them earlier this week and they seem to think nighttime is the time to be awake."

Whitney offered her friend a sympathetic look.

Ben walked into the kitchen interrupting their conversation, flashed them both a smile and reached into the fridge retrieving two beers. He leaned in and kissed Ever chastely, cupped his large hand over her belly, then flashed them both another grin and returned to the living room.

Ever shook her head, her face flushed, rosy and sweet.

Whitney looked at her friend with adoration. Ever was so much in love with her husband and seeing their interaction made her heart swell with happiness for her. In less than a year, Ever had found her happily ever with Ben and Whitney couldn't help but long for that too. Her mind drifted to Hayden. He was affectionate with her like that. Stealing little moments to acknowledge he saw her, cared for her, and loved her. *Would he take every moment to touch my belly if I were pregnant?* The possibility of having children with him drifted into her thoughts.

"Whitney, where did you go just now?" Ever asked, her hand on her hip.

Whitney laughed nervously and shook her head, breaking out of her daydream.

"Thinking of Hayden?" Ever asked, leaning against the kitchen counter, a knowing grin on her face. Whitney nodded and looked down at her hands, a smile curving her lips. "You know, Hayden is going to be an amazing dad one day, right?" Ever asked her, more of a comment than an actual question. "You want a family, don't you?"

"More than anything." Whitney replied with conviction, looking Ever straight in the eye.

"I know you and Hayden haven't been together long, but maybe you should have a talk about the future. Maybe discuss expectations and what you both want."

"Don't you think it's a little early for that kind of talk?" Whitney asked, raising her eyebrows in question. "We've only been dating a few months."

Ever pointed at her belly and the ring on her hand, then laughed. Whitney joined in on her laughter and nodded her head, acknowledging the quick timeline of Ben and Ever's relationship.

"I will bet you the farm that Hayden has thought of it already and is just waiting on you to catch up."

"You think?" Whitney asked wistfully.

"I know." Ever replied, rubbing her hand over her

belly. "Hayden is without question thinking about a future with you."

Whitney stared at Ever, taking in her words. *Was Hayden already thinking of their future together?* There was no question that they loved each other, but other than her daydreams and passing thoughts about what her future with Hayden could look like, she had not verbalized it to him. She feared voicing it would be perceived as too fast or just plain crazy. She was simply savoring the feeling of being wanted and cared for by a man for the first time in her life. *Was he ready to commit fully?* So many questions floated into her head all at once.

Ever stared back at her and cocked her head to the side, scrutinizing her. "Whitney, does a future with Hayden scare you?" she asked. "Considering everything you've gone through in the past."

"Honestly, no," Whitney answered with full certainty. "I feel excited about the possibilities."

Ever pulled Whitney in for a huge hug. "You deserve every happiness, Whitney."

Whitney opened her mouth to thank Ever when her friend grabbed onto her, and let out a painful cry, her hand grabbing for the countertop. Whitney held her up, Ever's face contorted in pain.

"Ben, come here quick!" Whitney shouted from the kitchen, trying to hold her friend up.

Ben rushed into the kitchen, Hayden and Bea close behind. "Sweetheart, what's wrong?" Ben asked, his face turning white with worry.

"I just got a sharp pain." Ever winced, breathing

through her teeth, her eyes darting frantically towards Ben.

"She suddenly doubled over." Whitney explained.

"We should take her to the ER." Bea answered as she led her to a kitchen chair, Ever holding her belly and wincing from the pain. "It could be nothing, but it's best to get checked out. Just take deep cleansing breaths, and Ben go get the truck started." Bea ordered, now in full nurse mode. "You and the babies are going to be okay." Bea soothed in a whisper, running a hand over Ever's belly. Ben sprinted out of the house, keys in hand.

Whitney and Hayden stood back clutching one another, feeling helpless as they watched Ben run back into the kitchen holding Ever's jacket. Bea helped her into the jacket and Ben effortlessly scooped her into his arms, carrying her through the kitchen and out the front door.

Bea peered around the corner to Hayden and Whitney. "I'm going to go with them, okay?"

"Of course." Hayden answered, his face pale with shock and worry at what had just happened.

"We're going to be close behind." Whitney replied, going into action mode cleaning up the food that had been laid out for them.

Bea nodded and bolted out the front door, the storm door slamming behind her.

Hayden stood there unmoving, his eyes wide and face pale as the snow outside. Whitney wrapped her arms around him in a comforting hug, meeting his concerned eyes, unshed tears forming. Her heart ached for the sensitive man she loved so much. "She is going to be okay." Whitney reassured him. "You heard Bea. She said it's probably nothing and taking her in was just precautionary. The babies are going to be okay."

* * *

HAYDEN AND WHITNEY pulled into the garage. It was after midnight, Christmas Day, and both were exhausted. The unexpected visit to St. Augustine ER resulted in bed rest for Ever, but thankfully both she and the babies were fine.

Turning on the Christmas tree lights; Hayden flopped onto the couch, patting the spot next to him. Whitney sank down, letting out a long exhale. "Well, that was the most eventful Christmas Eve I've ever had," she offered, snuggling into him.

Hayden nodded in agreement, putting his arm around her. They sat there together for a long time, mesmerized by the twinkling lights on the tree.

"Oh, I have something for you!" Whitney exclaimed, suddenly breaking their reverie. She popped up off the couch and reached down under the tree, retrieving a rectangular box.

"Aren't we exchanging gifts Christmas morning?" he asked as she set the box on his lap.

"Technically, it is Christmas morning, but yes, we are. This is just something cute and fun for us both," she offered. "A little Faris tradition."

Hayden smiled at her and started unwrapping the box, colorful paper flying. Opening the box, he laughed as he held up a pajama shirt, the front of the shirt reading, "On Santa's Naughty List." Whitney laughed and clapped her hands, grabbing the second pair meant for her. She held hers up, and it read "On Santa's Nice List."

Hayden blurted out a bountiful laugh and pulled her in for a hug. "Let's go put these on and maybe I will show you why I am on the naughty list," he teased, nipping her ear with his teeth. She squirmed and giggled as he chased her down the hall to their bedroom.

HAYDEN'S EYES OPENED GROGGILY, Whitney's hair fanned out on the pillow and now tickling his nose. He held back a sneeze and smiled. She was warm and soft, molded into the groove of his body. He loved waking with her, his little spoon. Hayden ran his hand over the dip of her waist and the curve of her hip, relishing the feel of her under his touch. His hand roamed over the curve of her backside and back around to her stomach, where his hand rested. Yesterday had been crazy, seeing Ever in such pain, the fear of trouble with her pregnancy, a real worry. His hand spread wide over Whitney's belly, his mind wandering. *What would it be like to feel a bump here? What would it be like to see Whitney carrying my baby?* Over the past month he had these thoughts many times. His desire to have a family coming to the forefront of his thoughts as his relationship with Whitney grew serious. *Is she ready to talk about the future?*

"Merry Christmas, Hays." Whitney whispered sleepily, breaking him from his daydream.

His hand still splayed on her belly, she intertwined her fingers with his.

"Merry Christmas," he replied, kissing her neck and nuzzling his stubbled chin against her cheek. She squirmed and wiggled back into him, her movements awakening his body with arousal. His hips instinctively meeting her with a slow sensual grind.

"A very Merry Christmas indeed," she said, feeling his hardness grow against her. "Do I get my first present now?" she teased guiding his hand under her shirt to cup her breast.

"I think that can be arranged," he replied, rolling her nipple between his thumb and forefinger. She moaned at his attention to her breast and turned her body to face him. Her hand roaming down to his manhood begging to be freed from his flannel pajama pants.

He closed his eyes and moaned as she slipped past the waistband and boldly took hold of him, sliding her hand up and down, making him slick and ready. Letting him go, she shimmied herself out of her sleep pants and climbed on top of him, straddling his hips. He reached between her legs running his fingers through her soft folds, making her impossibly wet. Positioning herself over him, she sank down, sheathing him fully inside the warmth of her body.

"Whitney, you feel so amazing, but gorgeous we need protection."

Whitney shook her head and, bringing her lips to his, whispered, "It's okay."

Hayden gazed up at the beautiful woman above him, so trusting and vulnerable. She wanted him with no barriers, nothing between them. He had never done this before, and he needed to know that she was truly okay with this. "Are you sure?"

"I'm on birth control. We're good," she replied, grinding her hips into him.

Her words and movement fueling his pleasure. He closed his eyes and let out a deep, approving groan. She circled her hips a few times, teasing him, then set a pace rising and falling with him meeting her movements. Feeling the familiar tingle of his climax start up his spine, he revelled in the feel of her tight heat surrounding him like nothing he had experienced before. Reaching between them, he teased at her centre, making her cry out with pleasure at the contact.

"Come for me, gorgeous," he commanded, feeling her walls grip him and tremors pulsate through her like waves. Her inner control was a marvel. He gave in to his release along with her. Their bodies shuddering and their sensual moans filling the room. Coming down from their intense mutual release, she collapsed on top of him, and they lay there connected for a moment, just savoring their connection. With the incandescent glow surrounding their joined bodies, Hayden felt emotions well up inside his chest and he swallowed down, a lump forming in his throat as he wrapped his arms around her tightly. Whitney had now given him all of her and she was the one and only woman he would make love to for the rest of his life. The overwhelming realization washed over him like a wave crashing against the shore and all he wanted to do was drown in this glorious feeling.

* * *

WHITNEY TOPPED off her cup of coffee as she made her way into the living room. Hayden had made them a delicious Christmas breakfast of his mother's famous French toast, which he told her was a Hastings tradition and now they were ready to open each other gifts. Hayden was already seated on the floor by the tree, reaching underneath to retrieve his gift for her. She took a seat on the floor across from him and crossed her legs. He handed a gift to her, and she reached under the tree, handing hers to him.

"I want you to go first." she said with an excited smile.

Obliging her request, Hayden ripped open the paper and gave Whitney a curious look as she gestured for him to continue unwrapping. He pulled out a piece of paper with information printed on it and he perused the printout, a slow smile tugging at his lips as he glanced up at Whitney with surprise.

"You didn't?" he asked, his eyes wide. "NHL Season tickets?"

She nodded, delighted by his reaction. "Yes, you get a select number of tickets before the season ends. You can take Ben or me or whomever you want to go with you."

He leaned in and kissed her softly. "This is far too generous!" he exclaimed. "Thank you."

"You're welcome." she replied, happily.

"Now I want you to open yours," he said, gesturing to the box in her hand. "It is not nearly as generous as your gift, but I hope you like it."

Whitney looked down, untied the bow at the top of the box, and lifted the lid. She gasped in surprise. "Oh,

Hayden, it's exquisite." She lifted his gift out of the box. Inside was a wooden box, carved intricately with a large star in the middle and bursts in the corners. The sides were carved as well, with stars in a unique pattern. She ran her hand over it, feeling the smoothness of the wood and the details carved into each star. The design was stunning.

"Did you make this?" she asked, searching his eyes.

"I did. I wanted to give you something handmade from me, to remind you of the night I told you I loved you," he confessed sweetly.

Her heart leaped out of her chest at his words, and tears filled her eyes.

"It's a treasure box," he explained, motioning for her to open it. "I figured you could put memories in there. It can be trinkets, photos, whatever you want," he continued. "I also put a message in there for you." He pointed to a wooden plaque inside the lid that said. "Because I love you. Hays."

She looked up at him, meeting his gaze, blinking through the tears now spilling over onto her cheeks.

"Do you not like it?" he asked, his brows knit together in question.

She nodded her head vigorously and swiped at the wetness on her cheeks with her hand. "I love it, Hayden. It is the most beautiful gift anyone has ever given me."

He breathed out in relief and smiled at her lovingly, his eyes full of raw emotion.

She set down the box and climbed into his lap, straddling his hips, and took his face into her hands. "You are the best gift I could ever ask for," she professed, then kissed him passionately, washing away any lingering doubt she had left.

Hayden Hastings was her forever.

The new year passed with Hayden and Whitney riding the bliss of their new life together. Whitney, having gained several new clients, was working from home on her laptop. Her phone buzzed with a text. Thinking it was Hayden, she picked it up, a smile on her face. Her smile quickly disappeared.

"Where are you, Whitney? Bitch, are you with him? I know you're with someone new. Slut. Always screwing around on me. You belong to me. Don't you know you have always been mine? No one else can love you like I love you."

Whitney read the text again, her face turning pale, her stomach falling to the floor. Feeling her lunch coming up, she scrambled to the sink and threw up, her body retching painfully as she emptied the contents of her stomach into the sink. Running the water, she washed away all evidence of her sickness and reached for a paper towel to wipe her mouth. *How can Paul still affect me this way?*

Since her move to Primrose, she hadn't so much as

heard a peep from Paul. And now this. Her head started to ache, and she walked over to the couch and sunk into the cushions. Closing her eyes, she tried to ward off the anxiety attack, which was rapidly building inside her. *Does Paul know about Hayden? If so, how does he know? All my social media is private, only friends can see my posts. Perhaps I need to double check my settings.* A mental checklist rapid firing in her mind.

Just then, her phone rang, startling her and causing her to drop it onto the cushion next to her. Recognizing the number as the property manager for her apartment building in Toronto, she answered it.

"Hi James! How are you?" she greeted, trying to steady her building anxiety.

"I'm fine, but I'm so sorry to tell you that your apartment was broken into last night."

"What?" Whitney asked in disbelief as she rose from the couch and started pacing, her stomach aching painfully again.

"Yeah, one of your neighbours noticed your door unlatched this morning. It was scraped up, looking like it was pried open. She reported it to me, and I called the police. They're up there right now. Are you at work right now? Were you gone over the holidays? I haven't seen you around the apartment for a while."

"I've been in Manitoba for the past two months," Whitney answered.

"Oh, that explains it. Whitney, this is a secure building, so I have no idea how someone could just break in. I'm going to go through the surveillance cameras with the police."

"Okay, I will fly out as soon as I can."

"It's not good Whitney, the apartment is trashed," he answered with sincere sadness in his voice. "Let me know when you're coming."

Whitney hung up the phone and stood there, holding it in shock. First the text, then the call about her apartment. Without question, Paul had something to do with the break in. She felt it in her gut. She needed to get to Toronto as soon as possible. With shaking hands, she dialed Hayden's number at work.

"Hastings Hardware."

"Hayden?" she asked, her voice cracking with emotion. "It's Whitney. I need to fly to Toronto. Something bad has happened."

HAYDEN AND WHITNEY exited the plane at Pearson International Airport and made their way to the luggage claim. Whitney had been quiet the entire flight, and Hayden ached painfully for her. He could see the worry in her eyes and wanted desperately to take this burden from her. Finding out what had happened, he immediately made arrangements so he could go with her. Whitney should not have to her deal with this alone and the thought of her ex-husband threatening her made him want to act as a protective shield around her. Paul would not get near Whitney.

They retrieved their luggage and hailed a cab to take them to their hotel. After dropping off their luggage, they headed to her apartment.

The property manager for her building met them at the front door of the complex. "Hey Whitney." he greeted, giving her a quick hug. "I'm so sorry you had to rush here under these circumstances."

Whitney gave him a sad look and gestured to Hayden. "James, this is my boyfriend, Hayden Hastings."

The men shook hands and James guided them to the elevator as he updated them on the situation.

"I've not touched anything. The police have dusted for fingerprints, looked for any evidence they may need, and did everything they can do right now. Your apartment just needs to be cleaned up. I'm not sure what your plans are for your lease coming up?" James asked, pressing the sixth floor button.

"I will not be renewing."

"Okay, then painting and patching will need to be done so I can rent it out on February 1st. I changed the locks, so here is the temporary key for you," he said, handing it over. "When you're done, you can just drop the key in the office mailbox."

They walked down the hall together and Hayden took Whitney's hand in his, giving it a supportive squeeze, letting her know he was with her through this. Whitney glanced up at him, so much emotion in her deep brown eyes.

"Let me know if you need me," offered James, turning to head back downstairs.

Whitney turned the key and opened the door slowly, apprehensive of what she might find. Immediately, Whitney gasped and her hand came over her mouth in shock. On the wall were the words, "Stupid Bitch." written in spray paint. Her couch was turned over, the cushions ripped and shredded, their stuffing strewn about the apartment. The bookshelves toppled and her books were torn and thrown around the room. She walked over to her kitchen and all her dishes, glasses and serve ware were smashed, piles of glass all over the hardwood floor. Her coffee pot was smashed, as were her small appliances she had on the countertop.

Hayden looked around in horror at the rubble that was left of her apartment. Rubble being the only way to describe the disaster before them. Whitney silently picked up a piece of a decorative glass bowl and looked at it sadly, then threw it aside in the pile of glass on the kitchen floor. Hayden felt tears prick his eyes, as all he could do is watch her, taking in all that she owned broken and destroyed. The scene was devastating, and Whitney was somber in her perusal of the damage. She walked slowly down the hall, stepping carefully over piles of her belongings to what he assumed was her bedroom. She stopped and stood pale faced in front of her bed. Not until he reached her did he see what she was looking at. Written across her headboard in spray paint was the word "SLUT". At that moment, Whitney crumpled to the floor, her knees giving out on her. Loud, frantic sobs, escaping her throat as her body convulsed with each piercing wail of anger, utter devastation manifesting outward with her other worldly cries. Hayden went down to the floor with her and lifted her into his lap, cradling her as she let go. She turned, burying her face in his shoulder, the sobs wracking her body violently. Hayden, shaken himself, couldn't hold back his own tears as he held her, so confused why anyone would do this to her.

* * *

Hayden and Whitney had been in Toronto for four days, cleaning, painting, and repairing all they could. Exhausted and with the final inspection done by the Property Manager, Whitney held a box of items she managed to salvage and took one last look at her apartment. A place she loved for the past five years and now it was time to say goodbye. Carrying her box of books and keepsakes that survived the ransacking of her apartment, she took one last look around, then closed and locked the door to her old life.

"Are you okay?" Hayden asked, putting his hand on the small of her back.

"I will be," she said, giving him a half smile. "These past few days have been a lot to deal with."

Hayden acknowledged her, leaning down to give her a chaste kiss and rubbed her back supportively.

When they had arrived and had seen the devastation, they paid a visit to the police station to give a statement and press charges against Paul. Whitney reported the threatening emails and texts she received from Paul and applied for another order of protection. They had already matched his identity with the surveillance camera and a warrant was out for his arrest. There was nothing more she could do for now but hope they would be able to apprehend him.

Hayden grabbed the box she was holding, and they made their way to the elevator. Setting the box down at his feet while they waited for the elevator, he pulled her into him for a hug as he rubbed her back and kissed her head affectionately. The elevator dinged, and the doors opened, and a tall, lanky man walked out. He wore a black bomber style winter jacket, a toque slung low, his head was down. Hayden caught his eye, an unsettling smirk on his lips. He nodded, acknowledging Hayden, their eyes meeting, then looking down quickly, he stuffed his hands in his pockets. Hayden grabbed the box and took a double take at the man now opening his apartment door, two doors down from Whitney's old apartment. Something about him felt suspect. His dark eyes, piercing, almost sinister. His smirk, not friendly, but showing a meanness that made Hayden's gut ache. A deep uneasiness enveloped him by the brief encounter as he followed Whitney into the elevator and to the waiting cab outside the apartment building.

BACK IN THEIR HOTEL ROOM, Whitney climbed into bed next to Hayden and nestled into his chest, her hand resting on his stomach.

"You're quiet. Something on your mind?" she asked, noting his mood change since they left her apartment.

Hayden took a moment to think through her question, then replied. "Yes, it's probably nothing, but do you remember that guy that got off the elevator when we got on at the apartment building?"

"Vaguely. Why?" Whitney asked, popping her head up to meet his eyes.

"There was something about him that seemed off." Hayden commented, furrowing his brows. "Was he a neighbour of yours?"

"No, I knew all my neighbours. I had lived there for five years and knew everyone. Perhaps he had just moved in?" she suggested with a shrug, as she laid her head back down and nestled into Hayden.

They both lay there a while in quiet contemplation, but Whitney could feel Hayden was still tense and deep in thought. Breaking the silence, Hayden asked. "Do you have a picture of your ex, Paul?"

"No, but I bet he has social media." she answered, sitting up and grabbing her phone. She combed through her phone for a few minutes and turned it to show Hayden. The profile picture of Paul before him. He had greying hair, thinning on top, and looked tall, thin and lanky in build. He enlarged the picture and surveyed his face for a moment. Dark eyes stared back at him, the same dark eyes he saw earlier today. He looked at Whitney, her eyes curious and imploring him for answers. Hayden looked up at her, his face paling as he spoke. "Whitney, Paul lives two doors down from your apartment. We need to call the police."

* * *

PAUL WAS ARRESTED that night and Whitney got the call that he was brought into custody. Through police questioning, they found out Paul had acquired the apartment two doors down from Whitney through a sublet and had been there since August of last year. He had been tracking her every move and when the police arrested him, they discovered hundreds of pictures of her taken as well as a notebook recording her movements. He had been stalking her and although they were not 100% sure of his intent, they found tape, rope, and tranquilizers in a duffle bag in his closet, which pointed to a potential abduction or worse. Whitney was instantly sick to her stomach.

Knowing he was now behind bars, Whitney was ready to go home. Her new home with Hayden.

Whitney walked into their house carrying her box of items from her Toronto apartment, and Hayden carried in their luggage. He tossed his keys on the island and put down the suitcases. Whitney put down the box and sighed.

"Come here." Hayden gestured, tapping his chest.

Whitney walked into his strong arms, so warm and comforting. She sighed again, feeling the weight of the emotion from the past week lifting off her shoulders. A chapter had been closed in Toronto and now a new chapter was officially opening. A feeling of love and gratitude swept over her, and she looked up at Hayden, meeting his concerned eyes.

"Thank you." she said. "I don't think I could have dealt with everything if I didn't have you there with me, holding me up. I love you so much."

Hayden offered her a tired smile and leaned down to tenderly brush his lips to hers. He was undoubtedly exhausted and the realization of what she had put him through over the past few days sat heavy on her heart.

The events of the past week, and her past in general, was a lot to deal with. Knowing that this incredible man who she was in a new relationship with would literally drop his life to come to her rescue when she needed him, was overwhelming. *Was this all too much for him? Would he wake up one day and say, I can't do this anymore? That it's all too much.* Part of her had faith that he would never do that to her, but part of her felt insecure and questioned if he could handle it. *Would he one day walk away?* The thought of not having him in her life made her emotions overflow and a cry inadvertently escaped her throat.

Startled, Hayden looked down at her, searching her face. "Are you okay?" He asked, brows furrowed with concern.

"Yes, just overwhelmed." she replied. "Can I ask you something?"

"Yes, of course, anything."

"I know I bring a lot of baggage with me, and I know this entire situation is far more than most can handle. Although you've been amazing through everything, I need to ask, aren't you scared?"

He looked into her eyes, searching for the meaning behind the question. "Yes," he confessed, "but not for the reason, you may think. I'm not scared of your past, any scars you carry because of your past, or helping you process through the events of this past week. Do I wish it never happened to you? Yes, of course. I wish you didn't have to go through what you went through."

"Then what scares you?" she asked, needing desperately to know.

"I'm scared of losing you," he answered, his voice

rough around the edges. "Knowing Paul had intent to abduct and physically harm you, or worse. That's what scares me." Whitney searched his eyes, seeing the fear within their depths. "Whitney, if something ever happened to you, if someone ever hurt you, I ...." he trailed off.

"I know Hayden." she finished, wrapping her arms around his neck and silencing him with a kiss.

In that moment, nothing more needed to be said. Hayden was accepting her past baggage and there was nothing he wouldn't do to keep her safe.

* * *

"YOU'RE THE BEST!" Ever exclaimed as Whitney passed her a plate with a cinnamon bun from the Eazy.

Whitney smiled, holding her own plate as she settled into their leather couch opposite from Ever. "How is the bed rest thing going?" Whitney asked, licking cream cheese icing off her fingertip.

Ever rolled her eyes and gave her an exasperated look. "It's exhausting. But anything to keep these two cooking." she said, rubbing her growing belly.

Whitney smiled, taking a bite of her cinnamon bun.

"So, I heard you had quite the impromptu trip to Toronto." Ever mentioned. "Are you going to tell me about it?"

Whitney put down her plate on the coffee table and looked up at her friend's curious eyes. "Where do I begin?"

Despite being so close to Ever, Whitney had never

shared details of her past marriage with her. It was not that she didn't trust Ever, but regaling her past was something uncomfortable to discuss and honestly something she didn't want to relive, even if it was part of her story.

"Start from the beginning." Ever replied.

Whitney sighed and spent the next hour opening up to her friend. As she did, she could slowly feel a weight lift off her shoulders. She shared about how she met Paul, their brief courtship, quick marriage, and the hardest part, the abuse. Sharing with Ever and seeing her reactions and wide-eyed compassion comforted Whitney, and she knew she was doing the right thing by telling her. Perhaps this was part of the healing process.

Concluding with the events of this past week, contemplative silence fell on the pair, Whitney knowing there was nothing more to tell and Ever rendered speechless.

"So, Paul is in jail now?" Ever asked. Whitney nodded. Ever let out a breath she seemed to have been holding and reached out to take Whitney's hand. "Now that I know everything, I think I have a better understanding of you, to be honest."

"How so?" Whitney asked, her eyebrow raised in question.

"I always felt like you never gave any of the guys you dated a chance," she explained. "You would regale me with all your tales of dating, but no one was ever quite good enough. You always found fault in them before they got too close to you."

Ever had hit the nail on the head. Whitney's marriage had made her fearful, and even though she believed in marriage and had an incredible example with her parents, the thought of getting too close to someone or letting them in was terrifying. Until Hayden, of course. A reflective smile came over her as she thought of him. Hayden, just by being himself, was helping her to heal from her past. Erasing all the bad memories of her previous marriage and making her consider a future with him.

As if reading Whitney's thoughts, Ever asked. "Have you and Hayden talked about the future?"

"No, not really, not yet," Whitney replied.

"What are you *waiting* for?" she asked. "Anyone with two eyes can see that you are perfect for each other."

Whitney knew Ever was right. She needed to confirm that she and Hayden were on the same page and the only way to do that was to bite the bullet and bring it up herself.

* * *

HAYDEN PEEKED into the main bedroom ensuite to find Whitney soaking in the free-standing tub. Two years before his parents passed away, they renovated the house putting in the new kitchen and his mother's dream bathroom with a huge shower for his dad, and at his mother's request, a big soaker tub.

Whitney had her blonde hair piled on top of her head in a messy bun and her black-rimmed glasses on, which she seldom wore, but he thought were sexy as hell. She held a romance novel in her hand and was encased in luxurious bubbles. The room was steamy, and the smell of lavender tickled his senses. The heat of the tub gave her an ethereal glow, and her milky skin was rosy and flushed. The swells of her breasts peeked out of the bubble filled water, instantly making him aroused at the sight of her. She looked gorgeous and he couldn't help but stand there, admiring her as she read her book, not noticing him standing at the entrance.

Finally, she looked up and her lips curved into an amused grin. "How long have you been watching me?" she asked, putting her book down on the vanity stool at her head.

"Long enough." He replied, leaning against the vanity counter and resting his hands on the countertop.

Whitney's eyes trailed down his body, stopping at the noticeable tent in his pants, and she rolled her eyes.

He flashed her a sexy grin, making her laugh. Her eyes turning serious as she pinned him with her gaze. "Hayden, do you mind if we talk seriously for a moment?"

Hayden furrowed his eyebrows and propped himself onto the countertop to take a seat.

"We need to talk about the future." Hayden nodded and met her gaze. "Where do you think our relationship is going?" she asked boldly, diving right in.

Hayden looked down, folding his hands in front of him. His pause making this important conversation draw out as he attempted to formulate the right words. *How can I fully express what I want with Whitney, without scaring her or making her feel like I'm wanting too much too soon?* Looking up, he investigated her deep, imploring chocolate eyes and all he could do was speak from the heart and hope for the best. He cleared his throat and nervously confessed. "I want forever with you."

"What does that mean, exactly?" she asked, needing clarification on his vague answer.

"It means that I can see you and I together in 50 years, a beautiful marriage and a beautiful life."

"Really?" she asked, looking at him and wrinkling up her nose. "50 years? I'm going to be so old and wrinkled."

"Old and cute," he corrected with a laugh, making her smile. "When I think of us and where this relationship is going, all I can think is that I want everything with you. What that ends up being, only time will tell, but what I can tell you is that I am 100% all in on this relationship."

Whitney smiled and crooked her finger, motioning him to her. He crouched down and leaned in to kiss her lips softly.

"What do you want from this relationship?" he countered, brushing a wet strand of hair from her face.

"The same as you. And your hot body, of course," she replied, giving him a sexy wink.

Hayden fell back on his butt laughing, then rose from the floor, reaching behind his back to pull off his shirt. "Got room for me in that tub?" he asked as he popped the button of his jeans and pulled them down, along with his boxers. Standing before her, naked and ripped with muscles, she licked her lips. "Always room for your sexy ass," she replied, batting her eyelashes at him.

He turned around and pointed at his taut backside. "You mean this one?"

Whitney laughed and slapped his butt with her wet hand, making the smack echo off the walls of the bathroom. She moved forward, making room for him to slide in behind her. He climbed in and lowered himself into the warm tub, his weight almost making the tub overflow. He leaned back on the tub incline and Whitney leaned back against him, her arms reaching behind her to encircle his neck. He ran his hands over her extended arms and down the side of her breasts and ribs making her shiver. He kissed her cheek as he wrapped his powerful arms around her naked body.

"Does it scare you that I want everything with you?" he asked, nuzzling her neck.

"No." Whitney answered quickly. "I've always believed in love and marriage, and it has always been something I've wanted. Having all of that with you doesn't scare me at all."

He smiled, her comment all the permission he needed. "Operation Forever" was officially activated.

CHAPTER 12

At the beginning of March, Whitney's parents insisted they come out to visit them in Arizona. Not having been to Arizona before, Hayden was excited and a little nervous at the prospect of meeting her parents. Although they had chatted several times via video chat, Whitney officially introducing him to her parents was a big deal to her and therefore an even bigger deal for him.

The dry desert heat assaulted them as they came off the plane at the Phoenix Sky Harbor Airport.

"Not in Manitoba anymore," he commented, taking Whitney's hand.

Whitney laughed and nodded her head in agreement as they made their way through the arrival gate and Whitney spotted her parents, her mother waving her arms to get their attention. Dan and Betty Faris were both in their early 60s, her father just under six feet tall, was broad and stocky in stature and wore a light blue golf shirt and khaki shorts. He had grey hair cut short to his head in a brush cut, hazel eyes and a full bushy Tom Selleck style mustache. Whitney's mother was an older version of Whitney. She had blonde hair cut into a bob, deep brown eyes just like Whitney's and a broad inviting smile. She was a beautiful older woman, and he couldn't help but think of what Whitney would look like when they were older. She wore a long flowing skirt and flower print tank top over her slim, svelte figure.

"Are you ready for this?" Whitney whispered, leaning into Hayden.

"As ready as I'll ever be," he answered as her parents approached them, emerging through a crowd of passengers.

"Dan and Betty! Nice to meet you." Hayden said, putting his hand out to shake Dan's. He took Hayden's hand in a death grip and gave it a good solid shake. Hayden couldn't help but laugh internally at his first attempt at intimidation. But he understood and respected it all the same.

"Well, this is Hayden!" Betty Farris chimed as she reached up to cup his face in her hands. "Look at those gorgeous blue eyes. Video chat does not do them justice!"

Whitney glanced at Hayden, and he caught her gaze. Amusement dancing across his face. Her mother wrapped her arms around him and squeezed him tight. No awkward pretense, just full-on affection.

"Oh, and all those muscles. My goodness." she commented, running her hands over his back.

Whitney rolled her eyes as her mother released Hayden from her hold, who was trying desperately not to burst into laughter.

"Hi Mom. Hi Dad." Whitney greeted, drawing their attention to her and giving both of her parents a big hug. "I've missed you both."

"Oh, honey, we are just so thrilled you two could spend the week with us!" Her mother cooed.

"We're happy to be here, too." Whitney replied.

Dan cleared his throat, fixed his eyes on Hayden, and gestured to the luggage claim, asking in a gruff tone. "Hayden, why don't we get the luggage?"

Hayden nodded, gave Whitney a quick wink and followed Dan to the carousel, leaving Whitney and her mother to hang back.

WATCHING THEM GO, her mother hooked her arm in Whitney's, and whistled under her breath, "Oh, my goodness, Whitney, Hayden sure is a handsome one."

"Mom, are you going to flirt with my boyfriend all week?" she teased, squeezing her mother's arm tighter.

"Perhaps, a lady is never too old to look at a handsome specimen like that." she winked, making Whitney laugh and shake her head.

Her mother was notoriously flirtatious, which, at times during her younger years, was a huge source of embarrassment. Now, as an adult, she couldn't help but appreciate her mother's boldness. She knew her parents, after 39 years of marriage, were still head over heels in love with each other and that her mother had no malicious intent behind any of her flirtations.

After a few minutes, Hayden and her father appeared through the crowd, rolling their two suitcases.

"Ready to go, sweet girl?" Her father asked, putting his arm around his daughter. Whitney reached up and kissed her father on the cheek, and gave him a nod.

* * *

THEY PULLED up to a modern townhome style condominium in a gated community. The yards were immaculately manicured and picturesque, and a golf cart was parked in front of their house.

"Welcome!" Betty announced, her arms spread wide, a huge smile on her face.

"Hayden, do you golf?" Dan asked, pointing over to his golf cart.

"Daddy, please don't drag Hayden around to every golf course in the area this week. We're here on a vacation together." She said with a roll of her eyes.

Dan let out a big huff making his bushy mustache puff out as he grabbed a suitcase. Hayden grabbed the other and answered. "I don't golf regularly, but I have always enjoyed it."

"Good!" Dan replied gruffly. "I will book us a tee time."

Whitney flashed Hayden a look of thanks as they followed her parents to the front door. Walking in, he was greeted by a spacious front entrance painted boldly in southwestern colors, the bright colors making it look more like a hacienda than a modern town home. Everything being on the main floor, Betty led them down a hallway into a large guest bedroom with a queen size bed, large dresser and a window looking out onto the back patio.

"You two can stay in here." Betty stated. "Do you two sleep together?"

"Mom!" Whitney scolded, her face turning red with embarrassment.

"Yes, Betty, Whitney and I share a bed," Hayden replied in a serious matter-of-fact tone as he glanced at Whitney, giving her a sly wink.

"Seriously, Mom, I'm 34 years old. Do you even need to ask?"

"Oh, I know Whitney, don't be so embarrassed. I know sex is an important part of a new relationship, so I just wanted to make sure the accommodations will be sufficient for you both. I would never expect you two to abstain the entire week!" she laughed, swiping her hand through the air as if the thought of them not having sex under their roof was completely absurd.

Whitney shook her head, her face an inferno, and Hayden's smile took over his face. *Betty Faris is a character.* Dan just huffed again and walked out of the room. *This is going to be such a fun week.*

"Okay, you kids settle in and meet us in the kitchen when you're done. Dad is going to barbeque steaks tonight!" Betty approached Hayden and reached up to pinch his cheek. "So handsome." She cooed as she floated out of the room.

Whitney collapsed on the bed, her arm over her eyes, her face and neck still red from her mother's comments. Hayden laughed and sat down next to her, patting her thigh. "I warned you." She commented, her voice muffled by her arm.

"You just said your mom is friendly and, at times, inappropriate," he replied with amusement. "But she is definitely next level."

Whitney groaned. "Are you going to run away screaming after a week of this?" she asked, removing her arm from her face and wrinkling up her nose.

"Not a chance. They're awesome. Seriously, your mom has no boundaries, but she means well and your dad, well, he is…"

"A hard ass?" Whitney inserted.

"Protective." Hayden countered. "Besides, I have something up my sleeve to win him over," he offered, giving her a confident glance.

"You do?" she asked, sitting up.

"I do," he confirmed, intertwining his hands with hers.

Whitney appreciated his confidence and felt at ease. If they were going to have a future together, he needed to know everything about her, including her crazy family. If Hayden was not having second thoughts after this week with her parents, he was, without question, a keeper.

* * *

"DAN, YOU GRILL UP A MEAN STEAK." Hayden complimented, sitting back in his patio chair and patting his stomach in appreciation.

"Thank you." Dan replied, placing his plate to the side. "The key is charcoal. It gives it more flavor."

"Good to know," Hayden commented.

"Let me get the dessert!" Betty added, getting up from the table.

"I'll help you, Mom." Whitney offered, rising from the table and stacking the dinner plates. She passed behind Hayden, gave his shoulder a squeeze and flashed him a smile.

The sliding patio door closed behind them, Dan cleared his throat and crossed his arms over his chest, giving Hayden an interrogating look as he asked. "So, what are your intentions with my daughter?"

Wow, he was going to go for it right out of the gate.

"Well, Dan, I love Whitney very much."

Dan squinted at him and asked gruffly. "And my daughter, does she love you?"

"I believe she does, yes."

He nodded his head and seemed to contemplate his reply, then spoke, "You know my daughter has been through a lot. I've seen Whitney at rock bottom after her first marriage ended." He explained. "I've seen her completely broken and very deeply hurt by her ex-husband. That's not something a father ever wants their daughter to experience."

Hayden nodded. "Whitney has shared her entire story with me. I was also with her in Toronto when she had her apartment broken into by Paul."

"Yes, Whitney told us about that," he replied with his mouth in a grim line as his gaze met Hayden's. "She said you were beside her through everything."

"I was. I couldn't let her deal with it alone. She needed me and I dropped everything to be with her." Hayden shared and let out a long-pained sigh. "It was a lot."

Dan looked off into the distance for a moment and cleared his throat. "Hayden, I believe you're a good man. I believe you're good for my daughter. She needs someone who puts her first and appreciates her for who she is. She needs someone she can depend on, who accepts her past and what that past has done to her. I can see you are that person for her." Dan shared, a smile tugging at his lips.

"Thank you." Hayden smiled back at him, then continued. "I plan on being there for her the rest of our lives if she will have me."

"So, I can assume then, that you want to marry my daughter?" Dan asked, his eyes boring into Hayden's.

"Yes, I do want to marry her. Your daughter is the most amazing woman I've ever met, and I love her very much. I want to give her a beautiful life. A life she deserves to have."

Dan nodded his head, his eyes glinting with approval fueling Hayden to ask his next question. "I want to ask Whitney to marry me, and it would mean the world to me if I could have your blessing?" Hayden asked, nervous butterflies taking flight in his stomach.

Dan looked off into the distance again, leaving an excruciating pregnant pause between them. Dan's gaze drifted back to Hayden and his mouth curved up into a broad smile, his hazel eyes twinkling with delight. "Yes, Hayden, you have my blessing."

* * *

"Mom, what do you think they're talking about?" Whitney asked, biting her nails as she watched Hayden and her father converse through the living room window.

"Oh, who knows!" her mother replied, waving off her question. "Hockey, golf, I don't know."

"It makes me nervous." Whitney winced.

"Don't worry Whitney, your dad's not interrogating him. He already likes Hayden; he's just doing his protective dad intimidation thing again."

Whitney rolled her eyes and glanced at her mother, meeting her gaze. "That's exactly what I'm worried about. He's going to scare Hayden off!"

Betty put down the cake server and offered her daughter an endearing smile. "Hayden loves you, I could see it immediately, so nothing is going to scare him off, including a little questioning from your dear old dad." Whitney glanced again at her mom, hoping she was right. "Now let me ask you something," her mother continued, pinning her with a stare. "What is holding you back?"

"What do you mean?" Whitney countered in question.

"Whitney, my girl, I can see the apprehension in your eyes. You love him, don't you?"

"Very much. It's just we've only been together five months and I already know I want to marry him and have his gorgeous blue-eyed babies." Whitney admitted. "Isn't that a bit too quick?"

"Oh geez, Whitney, your dad and I got engaged after six weeks! I knew within a week I was going to marry him, and we've been together for 39 years!"

"You never told me that!" Whitney exclaimed, stunned by this new piece of information.

"You never asked." Her mother shrugged. "If you love him, time doesn't have to play a factor unless you let it."

She put her arm around Whitney. "I can see plain as day that the handsome man out there loves you fiercely."

Whitney smiled and gave her mom a side hug. Picking up the cake and carrying it towards the patio, her mother glanced back at her. "Now stop worrying, overthinking everything, Whitney, snag that looker and get to work making me those gorgeous grand babies!"

HAYDEN AND WHITNEY had an amazing week with her parents in Arizona. Her parents fell in love with Hayden and by the end of the week they were referring to him as "son". Whitney rested her head on Hayden's shoulder on the flight back to Winnipeg, feeling happy and content. She sighed and intertwined her fingers with his.

"What is that big sigh about?" he asked, resting his head on hers.

"I am just so happy." She replied, giving his hand a squeeze.

"Well, that makes me happy," he replied. "I really enjoyed your parents."

"They loved you!" she exclaimed. "You even won over my dad, which is not an easy feat."

"It probably helped that I got us hockey tickets."

"Brilliant, by the way." She complimented, letting out a little laugh. "And my mom may be more in love with you than I am."

"She's hilarious." Hayden commented, an amused smirk on his face. "When we went to the community pool the other day, I was not sure if I should be flattered or disturbed."

Whitney rolled her eyes. "She patted your abs and counted them right there in front of everyone. I had to ask her to stop pawing my boyfriend."

"She is awesome." Hayden laughed.

Whitney lifted her head and looked up at him, her eyes full of adoration. "Thank you, Hayden, you're amazing. I love you."

He reached for her chin and lifted it, bringing her mouth close to his then brushed her lips softly with his. "I love you too, gorgeous!"

"Doors open!" Ever called out.

Whitney entered the farmhouse with two grocery bags in hand.

"Hey Mama! I have the stuff you asked for," Whitney replied, carrying the bags into the kitchen.

"Can you bring me the jalapeno chips and Nutella?" Ever yelled from the living room.

"Sure." Whitney replied hesitantly, grabbing both and joining her friend curled up on the couch.

Ever was stretched out on the couch, a stack of pillows behind her and a blanket over her legs. She wore an Aerosmith t-shirt that didn't completely stretch over her burgeoning baby belly and sweatpants, her mahogany hair in a messy bun at the top of her head. She looked swollen and tired, but beautiful just the same.

Whitney handed her the chips and Nutella and took a

seat at the other end, watching her friend open the Nutella jar and break open the chips. She dipped a chip in the Nutella and brought it to her mouth, closing her eyes in satisfaction. Whitney sat there, a bemused smile on her face. "Good?" she asked, raising her eyebrows.

"So good." Ever answered, popping another chocolate-covered jalapeno chip in her mouth. "These babies love some weird stuff."

Whitney laughed and pulled the large blanket over her legs as well, getting cozy on the couch with her friend.

"How was Arizona?" Ever asked between bites. "How are Dan and Betty?"

"Wonderful! They say hello and my mom is insisting on coming out after the babies are born, so she can..." Whitney held up her fingers, making quotations in the air. "Smell their sweet heads."

"Your mom's the best!" Ever laughed. "And how did they get along with Hayden?"

"Great! When my mom was not feeling him up or making inappropriate comments about our sex life, my mom was showing him off to her friends or fawning all over him."

Ever let out a huge guffaw. "Oh, my goodness, I wish I were there to see that! How about your dad?"

"Awesome! He and Hayden golfed, went to see a hockey game. They seemed to get along great." Whitney shared. "I honestly don't think it could have gone any better."

"That is awesome, Whitney. Meeting your parents is a big step in your relationship. Have you discussed the future yet?"

Whitney nodded.

"And?" Ever asked.

"We're on the same page, marriage, family, the whole thing."

"Someday you'll be my sister-in-law!" Ever squealed as she licked Nutella off her fingers.

Whitney smiled at the thought and continued. "I want everything with Hayden, but I need to settle my past first. I heard from my lawyer yesterday and Paul's trial has been set for mid April."

"What is the possible outcome?" Ever asked, her brows furrowing.

"Ten years for stalking and five for break and enter. I need a clean slate before I fully commit to Hayden, and I know if it were up to him, we would be engaged and planning a wedding already."

"I respect that. Close one chapter before opening another." Ever added.

"Exactly."

* * *

HAYDEN WALKED into the Eazy and spotted Ben in a corner booth. Making his way over, he slid in across from him and acknowledged the platters of burgers and fries on the table.

"Thanks for ordering my lunch for me. I don't have a long lunch today. Short staffed right now," Hayden explained as he dug into his meal.

"Yeah, no problem." Ben answered. "How was your trip to Arizona?"

"Amazing," Hayden replied through a bite. "Whitney's parents are awesome!"

"Big deal meeting the folks." Ben commented, leaning on the table, French fry in hand.

"It was, and I seized the opportunity to ask her father for his blessing to ask Whitney to marry me."

Ben sat back, with a huge grin on his face, crossed his arms over his broad chest and asked curiously. "What did he say?"

"He gave me his blessing." Hayden replied with a gratified smile as he bit into a fry.

"Wow, okay, when do you plan on popping the question?" Ben asked, picking up his burger.

"As soon as possible, I just need to think of a good way to ask," he replied. "It needs to be special and meaningful to us. I'm not sure how or where yet."

Ben squinted at Hayden, giving him his usual scrutinizing look as he questioned, "Is that what Whitney wants? A quick proposal. Doesn't she have a court date coming up regarding the stalking charges on her ex?"

"Yes, next week."

"Maybe you should slow your roll a bit then, Brother." Ben suggested.

"What do you mean?" Hayden asked, feeling frustration rise in his chest.

"I mean, Hayden, that you jump too quickly. Without thought at times. Have you even asked her what she wants?

"She says she wants to marry me," he replied, now getting agitated with his brother.

"I have no doubt about that, but does she want to

marry you right now? When she's still dealing with her ex-husband." Ben explained. "Perhaps let her get some closure on that situation before you pop the question."

Hayden hadn't thought of it that way. As annoyed as he was with his brother's line of questioning, Ben was right. *I need to find out where Whitney's head is at.*

* * *

"How was your day?" Whitney asked, peeking out of the ensuite, a toothbrush in her hand.

"Busy." he replied, giving her an exhausted look. "I have to arrange for my day staff, and I've not had time to do it yet."

Whitney emerged from the ensuite, crawled into bed, and leaned against the headboard.

"I need to make sure I have sufficient day staff for when we head to Toronto next week." Hayden explained.

"Speaking of that, I think I need to go alone for this trip." She said, meeting his gaze.

"Why?" he asked, turning to face her fully.

"I don't know how long this whole thing is going to drag out, or how long I'll be gone. First the court date, then sentencing. It could be one day or multiple days, depending on the judge." She explained, taking his hand.

Hayden nodded and answered with frustration in his tone, "And that's why I need day staff, so I can be there with you."

Whitney gave him a chiding look. "Hayden, last time we had to leave for Toronto, you had to close the store and when we went to Arizona, you were lucky Ben could step in and pick up the slack. With this trip being so unpredictable, you need to stay here. You can't just open and close your business every time you think I need you to rescue me."

Hayden squinted at her, his agitation growing with this conversation. "Ben, can step in again if I can't find staff before we have to leave."

Whitney let out a long breath, her words and explanations obviously not getting past Hayden's stubbornness. "You can't ask that of him. Ever is still on bed rest and they're going to be on baby watch. Ever is due early May and with twins being unpredictable, they could very easily arrive early."

"Then I'll close the store for a few days," he replied insistently, not wanting to budge.

Whitney rolled her eyes at him and met his gaze, irritated by his inability to reason. "Hayden, no. You have a business; your business pays your bills. It's not good for a business to just randomly shut down every time something comes up."

"Isn't that up to me to determine? Unless you don't want me to be there with you?" he asked, frustratedly climbing out of bed.

"That's not what I'm saying, but you need to be logical and listen to me," Whitney stressed, following him with her imploring eyes. "I can deal with this on my own. I don't need you to be my knight in shining armor right now."

Hayden gave her an exasperated look, shadows of concern in their depths. "Paul is going to be there, and you're likely going to have to take the stand. What if he tries something? What if he tries to talk to you or get close to you?"

"He's not going to be able to get close to me."

Hayden swallowed down hard, his eyes imploring her. "I can't let you deal with this alone."

"You can't let me?" she asked, her voice becoming shrill as her annoyance peaked. "Since when do you have a say in what I do? Before you, Hayden, I was a very independent woman and did everything on my own. I built my life back up after my marriage, with next to no help from anyone."

"I realize that, but why won't you just concede and let me be there to protect you?" he asked, raising his voice in frustration.

"Because this is something I need to do on my own," she whispered, tears of frustration welling up. "I need to face my past and get some closure."

Hayden stared at her and shook his head, then turned towards the door.

"Where are you going?" she asked in surprise.

"To watch TV. I'm suddenly not tired," he answered gruffly and walked out, closing the door behind him.

That night Hayden didn't come back to bed and, for the first time since they had been together, they didn't fall asleep in each other's arms.

Hayden hadn't slept properly in days, his argument with Whitney weighing heavy on his heart. Thinking back, he was aware of how he overreacted and that he made her cry, made guilt sit like a stone in his stomach. He had promised her he would never intentionally hurt her and although it was normal for couples to have their disagreements, the fact that he let his own stubbornness go that far, causing her pain, was unacceptable.

The hardware store door chimed, and he glanced to the entrance to see Bea Baxter enter. Spotting him, she walked over to where he was stocking a shelf and gave him a hearty punch in the arm.

"Hey there Hay Bale!"

"Hey Bea." he replied, in a wary tone as he feigned a smile.

Bea put her hands on her hips and cocked her head to the side, giving him a once over as she asked, "Why so glum, chum?"

Hayden shook his head, not wanting to answer her, and continued with his task of stocking the shelves.

"If you don't spill, I'm going to have to text Ben, or perhaps Whitney." Bea threatened playfully as she pulled out her phone, making a show of texting someone.

"Please don't," he answered. "Whitney's upset with me right now."

Stuffing her phone back in her pocket, Bea offered him a frown. "Trouble in paradise?"

"You could say that," he answered, walking back to the counter. "Whitney leaves for Toronto next week for the court hearing and insists I stay back here."

"Oh, so she doesn't want you to go with her?" Bea asked, leaning over the counter.

"She says she needs to deal with this on her own."

Bea stood up straight and put her hands on her hips. "I understand that. Did you get all protective caveman on her?"

Hayden met her inquiring eyes as he nodded.

Bea shook her head as she responded, "You forget I know you, Hayden. You fiercely protect those you love, whether they need it or not. Maybe you need to back off on this one. Whitney has been independent for a long time, and you need to respect that. Isn't that part of what you love about her?"

"Yes." Hayden answered, meeting Bea's gaze.

"Then trust her when she says she's got this."

Hayden knew Bea was right. Whitney wouldn't be facing this alone unless she needed to. Her words about facing her past echoing in his mind confirming it. He had to give her this. Give her a chance to stand strong on her own and find the closer she needed to move on with their future, no matter how hard it was to watch her go.

* * *

WHITNEY RUMMAGED through the closet and pulled out a few of her suits, laying them on the bed. The court hearing was three days away, and she was flying out tomorrow morning, so she had time to meet with her lawyer and get debriefed as to how this was going to go.

"Packing?" a deep voice asked from the doorway.

Whitney glanced up to see Hayden, looking exhausted and a little sheepish. Neither had gotten much sleep over the past few days. Hayden fell asleep in front of the TV each night and Whitney found herself tossing and turning in an empty bed. An invisible wall seemed to have been erected between them, and neither knew exactly how to cross it.

He approached her gingerly, the awkwardness thick between them. "Whitney, I'm sorry. I shouldn't have assumed you wanted me to come with you to Toronto."

Whitney looked up at him, her eyes sad. "Hayden, I understand your desire to protect me, but you can't protect me from everything. Some things I just must face on my own."

"I realize that," he said, meeting her gaze. "I love you so much, Whitney. I can't think of you being in that room with him. The thought of it is killing me."

"I know." She acknowledged, coming closer to him. "I appreciate that. This is simply something I need to do. For the first time in years, I feel confident and brave enough to face him and the reason I do is because of you." she confessed, her eyes holding his gaze as she stepped into his space and reached up wrapping her arms around his neck. "I need to close my past fully, so I can move forward with our future."

Hayden gave her an understanding smile and leaned down, kissing her gently. The feel of his lips on hers, something she had missed and craved over the past couple of days. Whitney pulled him in closer, deepening their kiss, allowing their deep commitment to each other to wash away all the tension from the past few days. Pulling her lips away from his, Hayden raised his eyebrow in question, flashing her his familiar frisky grin.

"Can we have make up sex now?" he asked with a coquettish waggle of his brows.

Whitney threw her head back in laugh as she replied, "I thought you would never ask."

WHITNEY'S TAXI pulled up in front of Burke Hatheway Law office in downtown Toronto. Gerald Burke, a family friend and her lawyer for her divorce years ago, knew her history with Paul. Although Gerald specialized in Family Law he was also well versed in Criminal and Civil Law and there was no one else she trusted more in this situation.

Checking in with the receptionist, Whitney went to take a seat, but before she could sit down, Gerald rounded the corner and greeted her with a big hug. "Whitney! It is so nice to see you! Are your parents well?"

"They are. I was just down in Arizona about a month ago to visit them."

"Wonderful. Let's go to my office and discuss the hearing. There are some interesting developments I want to go through with you."

Whitney followed him into his office and sat down.

Gerald took his seat and opened the folder in front of him. "Let's get to it. It seems Paul has changed his plea from not guilty to guilty on all counts, including Breaking and Entering and Criminal Harassment. With the surveillance footage, his fingerprints were found at the scene and with the evidence found in his apartment, his case was not strong enough for a not guilty plea. Also, because he moved into the apartment building in August and the order of protection didn't expire until September, he's in violation of the protective order, so we can charge him with that as well."

"So, what does that mean?" Whitney asked.

"It means we'll not be going to trial and there will just be a court hearing and sentencing. It means this is going to be over quickly and you can move on with your life," he answered, offering her a compassionate smile. "Paul is looking at a minimum sentence of 10 years without parole and a max of 20 years if found guilty on all charges, possibly more. He will get parole but will have to serve at least 10 years before that becomes an option."

Whitney looked down at her hands. Paul wouldn't be able to get near her again. "Will I be required to take the stand?" she asked, looking up at him.

"No, but as the victim here, you have the right to speak and say your piece if you want to."

Whitney glanced towards the window and reflected for a moment. *Am I brave enough to say what I need to say?* Knowingly, she looked up at Gerald and raised her chin. "I want the opportunity to speak."

* * *

WHITNEY WAS nervous as she paced the courthouse hallway. She felt her cell phone buzz in her hand and checked the message.

Hayden: You got this gorgeous. Remember how brave you are. Say what you need to say and come home to me.

Whitney smiled, hugging her phone to her chest. She loved Hayden so much. Even though he wasn't there with her physically, he was with her in spirit, giving her strength.

Gerald popped his head out of the courtroom and motioned for Whitney to come in. Whitney entered the courtroom, following Gerald to the front, and he gestured for her to take a seat to the right of him. A side door opened, the defence lawyer walked in with Paul following behind him, his hands cuffed and two court officers flagging the duo. Paul's eyes flitted over to Whitney, and she met his stare. His cold dark eyes froze her for a moment as she took in his thin, gaunt frame with the beginnings of a scruffy beard. So different from the Paul she remembered and yet the same. Darting her eyes away from him, she faced forward, remaining poised as Gerald leaned over to her and whispered. "We got this Whitney."

Whitney nodded and continued to look forward as the judge entered the room and they rose in her presence.

"The Honorable Justice Fields," the bailiff announced.

The judge took her seat.

"Please be seated." She said, before looking at the case file in front of her. "In the case of Paul Denski, the defendant and Whitney Faris, the plaintiff, with the charges of stalking, uttering threats, breaking and entering and failure to comply with a protection order, how do you plead?"

"Guilty, your honor," the defence lawyer answered on behalf of her ex-husband.

The judge nodded and opened the folder, perusing its contents for a few minutes, a restless quiet falling on the courtroom before she continued. "In reviewing this case and the evidence collected supporting these charges, it is the opinion of the court that a trial will not be necessary. Are we in agreement?" the judge asked, looking back and forth between both parties. Both lawyers answered, "Correct."

"Before I commence with sentencing, I want to give both Mr. Denski and Ms. Faris an opportunity to speak. Ms. Faris, you can go first."

Gerald touched her shoulder and gestured for her to stand. Whitney stood nervously wringing her hands, the judge nodding for her to start. "Thank you, your honor. I would like to address Mr. Denski personally."

"I will allow it. Go ahead."

Whitney took a deep breath and blew it out slowly as she turned towards the defendant's table, her eyes meeting Paul's from across the courtroom. His gaze was vacant and void of emotion. She held her head higher and spoke, her voice shaky but full of conviction.

"Paul, when we met 12 years ago, I was just a young, naïve woman, a woman that had her entire life ahead of her and wanted nothing more than to be cared for and loved. I wanted to have the love and devotion my parents had, and you promised that to me when you married me. In the years we were together, you did everything in your power to break my spirit. You called me horrendous names and blamed me for your shortcomings. You accused me of doing terrible things, things that you did many times during our marriage. You made me believe no one would ever love me. You tried everything you could to break me, but I want you to know that you didn't break me. I have risen above those years with you and have a bright, beautiful future ahead of me. A future full of love and true, honest devotion. And I hope you think about what you did to me and get the help you need so that one day, God willing, you'll become a better person." Whitney turned to the judge. "Thank you, Your Honor."

She sat down and the judge turned her gaze to Paul.

"Mr. Denski. Do you have anything to say?"

The defence lawyer turned to Paul, whispering to him, and turned back to the judge.

"My client has nothing to say."

The Judge took off her glasses and rubbed her hand over her face then looked up, addressing everyone in the courtroom.

"Mr. Denski, please stand." She announced. Paul stood as directed, and Whitney glanced at him, looking for any shred of remorse. *Nothing.*

"Although, this would normally be a case that would see trial due to the severity of the charges, I feel with the plea of guilty on all counts, jumping ahead to sentencing is the best course of action for all parties." Turning her attention to Whitney, the judge continued, "Ms. Faris, as a woman, I feel your words to Mr. Denski deeply. I've seen many cases over the years, and a case such as this is never cut and dry. However, in this case it needs to be." She turned back to Paul and continued. "Mr. Denski, I hereby sentence you to the maximum sentence of 20 years in prison for one count of stalking and one count of Breaking and Entering. An additional five years will be added to your sentence for uttering threats and two more years for breaking the order of protection against Ms. Faris. That is 27 years for the crimes you have committed. You will be eligible for parole in 15 years on the condition that you seek psychiatric help. Bailiff, please escort Mr. Denski out of the courtroom. This court is adjourned."

The gavel dropped, and Whitney seemed to finally wake from her nightmare. "Did that just happen?" Whitney whispered to Gerald, as he closed his file folder and stuffed it into his briefcase.

"It did, Whitney. It's finally over."

Whitney smiled, a tear escaping down her cheek. *It's finally over.*

HAYDEN COULDN'T WAIT to see Whitney. She had been gone for five days and he missed her so much he ached. Seeing the arrival doors open, he waited with bated breath as he held a bouquet of long-stemmed red roses. Her favorite.

Having video chatted with her last night, he knew the outcome of the court hearing and could see the relief on her beautiful face. She was finally free, and her ex-husband was in jail. That dark part of her life was now over and allowing them to finally move forward.

He glanced up to the top of the escalator and spotted her blonde head in the crowd. There she was, his gorgeous girlfriend, the love of his life. A huge, bright smile enveloped her face when she spotted him. Descending the escalator, finally reaching ground level, she ran towards him, dropped her carry on to the ground and jumped into his arms. Hayden laughed, trying to hold onto her and the bouquet of roses in his hand.

"I missed you, Hays." she declared, meeting his eyes, and crushing her lips to his. Her kiss softened as she melted into him, and he could feel all the tension leave her body. Pulling away, Hayden glanced around them, their kiss having made them a spectacle amongst the arriving passengers. "I don't care!" she exclaimed, showering his face with kisses. "I love you so much!"

"I love you too, gorgeous!" he laughed as she continued her onslaught of affection, and he slowly lowered her to her feet. "These are for you."

"They're beautiful." She mused, breathing them in deeply. "Thank you."

"Let's get your luggage and go home," he said with a coy grin. "I have plans for us."

She wrapped her arms around him and looked up through her long lashes as she asked. "Sexy plans?"

He stopped cupping her face and gave her a sensual

kiss right there in the crowd of onlookers. "Is there any other kind?"

* * *

HAYDEN AND WHITNEY LAY NAKED, tangled in their sheets, their bodies covered in a sheen of sweat.

"Now that's what I call a homecoming." She commented lazily, tracing figure eights on his chest.

Hayden's hand caressed down her back and over her backside, lifting her leg to curl over him. "I missed you," he confessed, kissing her head.

Whitney propped her chin up on his chest, looking up at him with a contented gaze. "I missed you too." Hayden overwhelmed her, in the best possible way and laying here, naked and satiated she knew that she never wanted to spend another day without him. He was hers and she was his, mind, body, and soul. "I can't imagine my life without you," she confessed, meeting his admiring gaze.

Hayden's lips curved into a sweet smile, and he flipped himself over and on top of her. Hovering over her, he dropped his lips to hers and kissed her tenderly, their love drowning them both and neither wanting to come up for air.

CHAPTER 14

$\mathcal{H}$ayden let himself into the Prairie Sky Farmhouse and closed the door behind him.

"Anyone home?" he called out.

"Up here!" he heard Ben reply. "In the nursery!"

Hayden climbed the stairs and turned the corner, making his way down the hallway. What was once Ever's room was now being transformed into a nursery. Entering the room, he saw Ben wearing an old pair of paint splattered sweatpants, had no shirt on and held a roller brush in his hand. Ever sat in a plush rocking chair, her feet up on an ottoman in the corner, a glass of ice water in her hand, admiring her husband and his handiwork. She was perfectly round, her enormous belly peeking out of her too small t-shirt that read, "Pregnant as a Motha." and a coy smile was painted on her lips.

Hayden chuckled at the scene in front of him. "Am I interrupting anything here?" he asked, looking from Ever to Ben and back to Ever, still eyeing up her husband.

"Yes, you're interrupting my sexy painter fantasies." Ever replied, biting the corner of her lip and giving Ben a coquettish wink.

Hayden let out a huge guffaw and looked at Ben, who waggled his eyebrows at his wife and continued to roll the cheerful yellow paint onto the wall.

"How are you doing, Ever?" Hayden asked, returning his gaze to her.

"I'm good, still cooking these little turkeys. The longer they stay in the oven, the better. So tired of being huge, though," she confessed, rubbing her giant belly. "Only three more weeks."

"That's really good!" Hayden exclaimed. "Don't twins usually come early?"

"Could be any day now," Ben replied, flashing him an excited smile.

"Good, because I think it is time to give you your baby gifts."

"The cribs?" Ever asked, clapping her hands together in excitement.

"Yes, they're on the truck now," he answered, giving Ever a sweet smile. "Ben, can you help me carry them in?"

Ben put down the roller brush and grabbed his T-shirt.

"You stay here, okay," he said to Ever, leaning down to kiss her softly.

Fifteen minutes later, Hayden and Ben had two hand-made cribs inside and up the stairs. Ever's eyes widened at the sight of them, and Ben offered her his hand, helping her out of her chair to take a closer look. Waddling over, she ran her hands over the intricate carvings on the headboards and smiled, pure joy on her face. "Hayden, these are incredible."

Hayden glanced down at his handiwork. Carved into both headboards were cute farm animals, horses, cows, pigs, chickens, and sheep. Each headboard had a spray of daisies carved into the peak. "When Ben told me you were going to eventually paint a farm scene in the nursery and you don't know if you are having boys or girls, I thought farm animals carved into the headboards would be appropriate."

"Hayden, the detail is amazing." Ben complimented, taking it all in. "Brother, you're seriously talented."

"You're an artist, Hayden." Ever added, giving him a side hug as she continued to inspect them. "Thank you so much."

"Anything for my first nieces or nephews!" he exclaimed. "Maybe someday I'll build my child a crib, too."

Both Ben and Ever's eyes flitted towards him at the same time and Ever flashed him a huge grin. He knew he was putting the horse before the cart, but he wanted a family, and that one day he would have one with Whitney.

* * *

ONE WEEK LATER, on an unseasonably warm spring day, Ben and Ever welcomed twin girls. Although they were small, both little girls were healthy.

Hayden and Whitney, eager to meet the sweet bundles, knocked lightly on Ever's hospital room door.

"Are you okay with two visitors?" Whitney asked, peeking into the room holding a bouquet of daisies for

Ever, followed by Hayden holding two pink bunnies for his nieces.

"Yes, come in." Ever welcomed, her face tired and flushed, but radiant with happiness.

Bea was there, doting on Ever still in her scrubs, having been on shift when Ever came into labor and delivery and Whitney went to Ever's side, giving her a huge hug.

Hayden took in his brother happily holding his identical twin daughters in his arms and raw emotion quelled in his chest as he approached them.

"Hayden, these are your nieces; Violet and Poppy." Ben said proudly, beaming down at his daughters.

Whitney looked at Hayden, his eyes glossing over with tears. "Can we hold them?" Whitney asked, approaching Ben.

Ben nodded and Whitney reached out to take the bundle on the left, then Ben gently set the right bundle in Hayden's arms. Hayden looked down on the most perfect, most beautiful baby he had ever seen. She was so tiny, with a button nose and cute bowed lips. Her eyes opened sleepily, and he swore his heart grew ten sizes bigger.

"Who do I have here?" Whitney asked, cuddling the sweet baby to her chest and staring down at her adoringly.

"That's Violet Everley." Ever answered.

"And you have Poppy Grace." Ben added, meeting Hayden's tear-filled eyes.

"Grace after Mom?" Hayden asked, searching his brother's gaze. Ben nodded, a nostalgic smile tugging at his lips.

Hayden looked down again at his adorable little niece and over at Whitney, who was transfixed on Violet. She glanced up, her face full of joy, and their gazes met in silent agreement. Someday soon this would be them.

* * *

Hayden met Dan and Betty at the front door. Whitney had been working in the city and had picked up her parents from the airport afterwards. Now having her own vehicle, she could come and go when she needed to and allowing her to meet more frequently with the artists she represented.

"Oh, Hayden, you handsome devil! Come over here and give me a hug," Betty exclaimed as she abandoned her luggage and walked into Hayden's arms. "She hugged him tightly and placed her hand on his stomach. "Oh, my goodness, do you have an eight pack now?"

Hayden laughed as he glanced at Whitney, who was already rolling her eyes at her mom.

"Just the six still, Betty, but I'll let you know if I add any more," he replied with a chuckle as he acknowledged her father. "Dan, nice to see you again too. How was the flight?"

Dan let out a huff, causing his mustache to puff out. "Fuller than a clown car," he replied. "We were packed in there like sardines."

"You just hate to fly, Dan." Betty scolded, waving her hand to dismiss his comment. "Stop your complaining. It was a perfectly pleasant flight."

Whitney shook her head and laughed. "Mom and Dad,

let me show you to your room and then I'll give you a tour of the house."

"That sounds lovely, dear." Betty cooed.

Whitney led them down the hall to the guest room, their rolling suitcases behind them. Hayden went into the kitchen and pulled out a charcuterie platter Whitney had put together earlier in the day, a bottle of wine and two beers.

Hayden could hear Whitney give them a tour of the main bedroom and her mother's gasp at their large four-poster king size bed.

"Do you really need that much room to make love?" she asked loudly, her voice carrying through the house.

Hayden shook his head and chuckled, imagining the shade of red Whitney's cheeks were at her mother's comment. Finally, they came back down the hall and into the living room, spotting him in the kitchen.

"You have a lovely home!" Betty complimented taking a seat at the island and making herself comfortable.

"Thank you. I grew up here. The house is only two bedrooms, but once we got older, Ben and I had our rooms in the basement, which is fully finished. I would like to put an addition onto the house one day, maybe add a few more bedrooms. I have five acres, so lots of room to play with."

"Sound like a big project. But I can see how you could do it." Dan added.

"More bedrooms? Does that mean you and Whitney plan to fill them?" Betty asked, her eyebrows raised in question.

Whitney laughed nervously. "Mom, please simmer down. We'll have babies when the time is right."

"Need to get married first." Dan added with a clearing of his throat. "Don't rush these kids, Betty."

"Oh stop!" Betty chided Dan. "When we got together all you wanted to do was make babies! You were hot to trot day and night!"

Whitney's hand went over her eyes. "Mom, can we please not talk about you and Dad's sex life?"

Whitney tentatively glanced up at Hayden, who was trying to hold back his laughter as he suggested, "Why don't we go sit out on the deck in the back? It's a warm night and I have some ribs I've marinated for dinner tonight."

"Sounds delightful." Betty sang out happily as she grabbed the bottle of wine.

"I'll be right out," Whitney informed as her parents went out the patio door to the deck.

When they were out of sight, Whitney buried her head in Hayden's chest and groaned.

"Hot to trot," Hayden repeated, his deep laugh escaping.

"Its almost like a competition for her. How many inappropriate comments can I make in the span of 20 minutes?" Whitney laughed, shaking her head. "Well, that's my mom."

"I love them, inappropriate comments and all!" Hayden declared, handing her two wine glasses as they slipped out the door to join them.

* * *

BEN and Ever's baby shower was to be held at the Primrose Community Centre and had become a town wide affair. Everyone wanted to see the Hasting twins and bring their well wishes to the happy little family.

Ms. Lynette, the town librarian, and good friend of Ever's late father; Hardin Wolton was organizing the event, and the centre was a bustle of activity.

Hayden, Whitney, along with her parents, entered the building and were immediately greeted by Ms. Lynette. Her silver, perfectly coiffed hair was pulled back the way she always wore it, and today she wore a flouncy polka dot pink and white dress and a pair of bright pink cat eyeglasses. Her blue eyes sparkled with excitement.

"Hayden, darlin'! I am so glad you're here! And Whitney, it's so nice to see you again! I hear you've taken this handsome guy off the market!" Ms. Lynette exclaimed happily. "I could tell at Ben and Ever's wedding that there was a spark there! Glad Hayden had the good sense to snap you up!" she said to Whitney with a wink.

Ms. Lynette was the town gossip and little, if anything, got past her. If you wanted info on anything or anyone, she had it.

"Hi, Ms. Lynette. This place looks wonderful and very pink!" Whitney complimented, taking in the room.

The large space of the community centre was an explosion of pink with pink and white streamers hung from the ceiling, pink and white striped tablecloths dressing the round tables and huge balloon bouquets with sparkly pink and white balloons atop each table. Violet and Poppy's names were displayed on a sign with huge scrolled, glittery pink lettering on the back wall.

There was no mistaking this shower was for a pair of baby girls.

"Ms. Lynette, these are my parents, Dan and Betty Faris." Whitney introduced, gesturing to them.

Ms. Lynette shook both of their hands and gave them a warm, welcoming smile. "I'm so glad you could be here. Please come in, find a seat, the gifts go over there and help yourself to some food." She informed, leading them further into the busy room. "Ben, Ever and their sweet little flowers are just over at the big table over there." Ms. Lynette gestured, then excused herself, rushing off into the kitchen.

Ben spotted them and gave them a wave as they made their way over.

"Dan and Betty!" Ever exclaimed, giving Whitney's parents a hug. "I can't believe you came all this way for our baby shower."

"Oh, we wouldn't miss it, dear!" Betty exclaimed. "You look beautiful Ever, where are your little sweethearts?"

Ever gestured to Ben, who had a baby in each arm.

"This is my husband, Ben Hastings, and our daughters Violet and Poppy."

Betty's eyes widened as her gaze trailed up to Ben, who towered over her.

"Oh, my goodness, Ever! You married yourself a lumberjack!" she exclaimed, giving Ever a look of approval before turning back to Ben and fixing him with a smile. "You are strikingly tall and so handsome!" she exclaimed. Ben's face instantly turned about as pink as the dresses Violet and Poppy wore. "And strong, oh my," she went on brazenly, reaching to feel his large bicep.

"Nice to meet you both," Ben greeted, an amused smile curling his lips. "Who would you like to hold Violet or Poppy?"

"No matter to me. I've been waiting to get my hands on one of those cuties!" Betty exclaimed, clapping her hands excitedly.

Ben handed her Violet, and Dan stepped forward and cleared his throat. "May I hold Poppy?"

Ben smiled and nodded, handing his other daughter to Dan. Dan's smile grew wide, his thick bushy mustache stretching across his face as he held the baby. Whitney could feel her heart swell at the sight. *Would he be holding his grandbaby soon?* The more that thought went through her head, the more she knew that's what she wanted.

* * *

THE AFTERNOON ROLLED by with a flurry of presents, food, laughter, family, and friends. Ever and Ben were showered with anything they could need and more for their baby girls. Whitney couldn't help but take in the generous community she was now a part of. Having been a city girl her entire life, she had plenty of friends but had never felt a sense of community like that in Primrose. Witnessing the love that surrounded Ben and Ever, Whitney knew this was the place she wanted to settle down and grow her family in. Her family with Hayden. The thought of marrying him and having a family together was what she thought of when she woke and every night when she went to bed. Now, with her past locked away, she couldn't stop the flood of thoughts for their future. She wanted to be

Hayden's wife, the mother of his children, and she didn't want to wait any longer for their future to begin.

"Deep in thought?" Ever asked, as she took a seat next to Whitney.

Whitney smiled and nodded. "Where are the girls?"

"Both sleeping. Hayden is holding Poppy, and I have no idea where Violet is right now. They've been passed around so much. Not surprised they're both passed out. It's been a busy day!"

Whitney glanced over to Hayden who beamed, holding his niece as he talked to Bea. Whitney could feel her ovaries quiver at the sight.

"Hayden's a natural." Ever commented, acknowledging Whitney's longing gaze on Hayden. "You've been thinking about having a family of your own, haven't you?"

Whitney whipped her head towards Ever and her eyes softened. "How could I not? Look at him," she commented, gesturing to Hayden cooing at Poppy. "Hayden is going to be an amazing father."

"I want that for you, Whitney." Ever shared, taking her friend's hand. "Why not start now? I mean, not everyone does things in order and you and Hayden love each other very much. Seems like a good foundation to me." she shrugged. "Plus, you said it yourself, you two do things backwards so maybe starting a family now is a good idea."

Whitney took in her friend's suggestion and replied, "Call me traditional, but I want to be married first. And it doesn't need to be fancy either. I would literally get married in the middle of a field, just the two of us, I don't want or need a big wedding."

"Why don't you do that, then?" Ever asked.

"What do you mean?"

"Literally get married in the middle of the field. Hayden doesn't care either if you have a big wedding or not. I overheard him talking to Ben the other day, and he told him he would marry you tomorrow if he could. Any place, anywhere."

Whitney's mind started spinning and a crazy but exciting idea popped into her head. She turned to Ever and met her gaze. "What are you doing tomorrow night?"

* * *

HAYDEN CLIMBED into bed and took in Whitney, who was leaning against the headboard, her glasses on, reading a book.

"Have I told you how I love your sexy librarian look?" he asked, flashing her a coquettish grin.

"Yes, Hays, many, many times!" she laughed, setting down her book on the end table.

She climbed on top of him, straddling his hips, and replied with a sexy rasp to her words. "But you can tell me again."

He groaned and pulled her in for a scorching kiss. Breaking their embrace, she looked at the devastatingly handsome man she loved more and more each day.

"I am ready." she stated with conviction as she looked deep into his eyes.

"For?" he asked with a smile, curiously searching her gaze.

Whitney climbed off him and off the bed, going into the ensuite. Hayden sat up and waited for her to return, confusion on his face. She returned with something in one hand and the bathroom trash can in the other.

"What are you doing?" he asked, his eyebrows raised in question.

"Hayden, this is my birth control." She held up a thin container. Then she raised the trash can to show him. With a motion, only to be described as a slam dunk, she threw the pills out.

"I am ready." she repeated as she put down the trash can and crawled back onto the bed and over Hayden. "I want to have a baby."

"Now?" he asked, his eyes twinkling with excitement.

"Yes!" she declared. "I know I said I wanted to wait till we are married, but I say screw it! Let's do it!"

Hayden laughed and reached out to cup her face with his hands. His eyes staring deep into hers as if he was searching for any shred of doubt or perhaps a hint of insanity. Only complete surety shone back at him. His own dreams and desires reflected in her beautiful brown eyes.

"You know Whitney, I never do anything half-assed," he said, pulling her nightshirt off, exposing her body to him.

"Oh, I'm counting on the full ass, and you're big..." he put his finger over her lips, halting her words.

"Kiss me, dirty girl. Let's make a baby."

CHAPTER 15

"Ever, do you think this is crazy?" Whitney asked, sitting at the kitchen table of Prairie Sky sipping Sun Tea and watching Violet sleeping in her bouncy chair.

"It's totally crazy!" Ever answered as she patted Poppy's back to soothe her. "But it's so incredibly romantic, too!"

Whitney smiled excitedly. "I can't believe I'm doing this. Are you sure Hayden has no idea?"

"100%. Ben and Bea are in cahoots with us and Mr. Estes, the marriage commissioner, of course," she replied in reassurance. "We'll ensure your parents are there and between Bea and I, we have made all the arrangements set up and ready to go."

"Hayden and I just need to show up, but how do I get him out there?"

Ever smiled, her eyes twinkling with delight. "Trust me, that part is already taken care of."

Whitney got home and found the house abnormally

quiet. She took off her shoes and peeked into the living room, seeing no one in the kitchen. *Where is Hayden? Where are my parents?* Walking into the kitchen, she opened the back door. No one was on the back patio. She heard Hayden's truck pull into the garage and leaned on the counter, waiting for him to come in.

Hayden came in and spotted her waiting there for him. "Hey gorgeous! I just dropped your parents off at Prairie Sky." he informed, making his way into the kitchen. "Ever asked your mom to help her organize the girls' closet as they got so much stuff from the baby shower and Ben was going to give your dad a tour of the farm. They invited them for dinner too, so you and I have the rest of the day all to ourselves." Hayden said, rounding the island and swooping Whitney into his arms. "What to do?"

Whitney squealed as he nibbled at her neck and growled in her ear. "Hayden, now?" Whitney asked with a giggle.

He waggled his eyebrows and carried her towards the bedroom. "We need to take every opportunity we can, now that your mom can't walk in on us," he laughed, entering their bedroom and throwing her onto the bed playfully. His hot, muscular body covering hers.

"We need to invest in locks on the doors next time they visit." Whitney added, her face turning red. "Seriously, no one needs to walk into someone's private bedroom to ask if we want eggs or pancakes for breakfast."

Hayden laughed. "Especially when I am being woken up by my frisky girlfriend."

Whitney covered her face. "I need therapy."

"I can't help you there, but how about a shower? I was thinking we could go out tonight. We haven't gone on an actual date for a while. How about dinner and a moonlit drive?"

"Sounds fantastic. Meet you in there?" Whitney asked.

"Sure," he replied, rising from her and stripping off his clothes. She watched as he padded naked into the ensuite.

When she heard the shower start. She grabbed her phone and sent Ever a quick text.

Whitney: "I think I can get Hayden there on time. Nice idea to get my parents over there!"

Ever: "Brilliant right? Hayden still has no clue! See you at 10 p.m.!"

"Are you joining me, gorgeous?" Hayden called from the shower.

"Yes!" Whitney rose from the bed, lifting her shirt over her head, her mind reeling at the surprise she had in store for Hayden.

* * *

WHITNEY CAME out of the ensuite, a cloud of steam following her. After an amorous shower with Hayden, she kicked him out so she could wash her hair and get ready for their night out. Makeup applied and hair pulled up back in a twist, she noticed a large white box on the bed with a note on top. Beside the note was a dozen red roses. Hayden loved any opportunity to treat her with her favorite flower and seeing another gorgeous bouquet made her heart swell with love. Picking one out of the bouquet, she brought it to her nose, taking a deep inhale.

Its sweet fragrance filled her senses, and she closed her eyes, imagining Hayden's eyes filled with tears when she revealed her surprise. Hayden was such a romantic, and she hoped her plan would be everything he had ever dreamed of and more.

Picking up the note on the box, she opened it and it read: *Something beautiful for the most beautiful woman in the world. I hope you like it.*

Reaching for the ribbon holding the white box together, she opened it slowly, lifting the lid and peeling open the tissue paper. Wrapped delicately in tissue paper was a lilac lace cocktail dress. She pulled it out of the box and held it up to her. It had spaghetti straps, a plunging neckline and low back. The lace was an intricate pattern of flowers and vines with a satin underlay. It was exquisite. Eagerly Whitney slipped into it, the dress hugging her curves and extenuating all the best parts of her body including her shapely toned legs. She could not think of a more perfect dress for this special night.

Retrieving a pair of strappy silver high heel sandals and a purple shawl she used for Ever's wedding from the closet. She added silver crystal earrings with a matching bracelet to complete her outfit.

Whitney took in her reflection in the mirror and smoothed her hands down on the dress nervously. This was it. Last year at this time, she never would have dared to dream that this day would come. Never did she think someone like Hayden would sweep her off her feet, show her what true unconditional love really was, and give her a second chance at the life she always dreamed of. Feeling beyond blessed, a quell of emotion rose in her chest as gratitude washed over her. Pushing back happy tears, she took one last nervous breath, squared her shoulders, and walked out of the bedroom to meet the man of her dreams.

* * *

HAYDEN LIFTED his eyes from his phone and went slack jawed. Every time he saw Whitney he marveled at her beauty, but tonight standing in front of him cascading in lilac lace, her golden locks swept up, showing her long silky neck. She took his breath away.

"You are…seriously I have no words, Whitney." he said, his expression one of awe as his eyes drifted over her.

"Hayden Hastings has no words. This may be a first." she teased, cocking her hip to the side.

Hayden rose from the kitchen stool and approached her, taking her hands in his. "You are the most gorgeous, stunning, absolutely knock me on my ass with your beauty, woman I've ever seen."

Whitney laughed and reached up to brush her lips to his. "Thank you for this amazing dress. It fits me perfectly."

He gestured for her to spin to give him a full 360-degree view, then feigned a heart attack.

"Stop!" She laughed, then gave him an approving look over of her own. "Now you look like a million bucks. I love this suit!" she complimented as she reached up to straighten his collar. "Is this from Ben and Ever's wedding?"

"It is. Or as I like to call that night, the night I made out with my girlfriend behind a barn," he replied, giving her a sexy grin.

"I wasn't your girlfriend back then," she corrected, wrinkling her nose at the memory.

He leaned down and kissed her gently on the nose. "That is true, but you already had my heart."

Whitney met his eyes; deep blue pools she knew she could drown in forever. At that moment her stomach growled loudly.

Hayden laughed and kissed her softly. "Let's head out for dinner."

Hayden had made reservations at a bistro on the outskirts of St. Augustine. The atmosphere was trendy but formal, with elegantly dressed tables, soft candlelight, and lush seating. Hayden took a seat across from Whitney and their waiter set down their menus, taking their drink orders to start. Leaving them with the menus, Hayden reached out to take her hand in his. He rubbed her ring finger with his thumb and glanced down at their hands. A nostalgic smile tugged at his lips as he looked up to meet her eyes dancing in the soft flicker of the candlelight.

"You are so incredibly beautiful, Whitney. How did I get so lucky?"

Whitney stared at him dreamily and he felt his heart flutter as a radiant smile curved her lips. "I ask myself the same thing." she answered simply. "I love you, Hays."

He leaned in, bringing her hand to his lips. "I love you too, Whit."

The waiter returned with their drinks, a glass of

cabernet for Whitney and an old fashioned for Hayden. They both ordered steak with side salads and settled into conversation about their time together.

"Can you believe it has been seven months since we started dating?" she reflected. "Is it strange that it feels longer?"

"Not at all. I mean, we've had a lot happen in seven months. You had to pivot your career and made a huge move to another province."

"We fell in love, officially moved in together, and I could finally lock up my past and throw away the key," she added.

"Ben and Ever had the most adorable little girls." Hayden said proudly. "I still think it's going to be hilarious watching my big brother be a girl dad. Those girls are going to have him wrapped around their little fingers."

They both chuckled at the vision of big old Ben at the mercy of two sweet faced and innocent little girls.

"Seeing you with them may be the hottest thing I've ever seen." Whitney commented, wiggling her eyebrows then offering him a soft smile. "You're going to be an amazing dad."

Hayden's heart soared with her words, "I hope so. I had some pretty great examples growing up. My dad was the best, and I know he would be so proud of Ben right now. I sometimes wish they were still here with us."

Whitney offered him a resigned smile and gave his hand a squeeze. "They are though. I truly believe they are up there cheering you and Ben on. They're watching Ben and Ever navigate a new marriage and parenthood and they are watching you and I fall in love."

Hayden met her gaze, emotion brimming on the edge as he added, "My mom would have loved our love story. She was a hopeless romantic like me. I know there were times that my dad and her would struggle, but one thing that always remained strong was their deep love and devotion to one another. I believe we have that kind of love, too."

"I agree. Marriage and life in general, is not always going to be a bed of roses, but if we stand by each other, we can overcome anything. I truly believe that," she said. "Look at what we already have overcome."

Hayden nodded, their journey full of obstacles and yet here they were together, having made it to the other side of each one. "I believe that too," he agreed.

"I mean seriously, how many couples can say they have overcome a stalker, a break and enter and a court hearing?" she asked, an ironic laugh escaping her lips.

"Check, check and check," he answered by drawing checkmarks in the air.

"And you were there supporting me through it all. Even when I needed to face it alone, I felt you were there with me, giving me the courage I needed to get through it." she expressed, meeting his gaze, unshed tears hovering on the edge. "I'm a stronger, more confident version of myself because of you, Hayden. Thank you."

"No thank you," he answered, his voice cracking with emotion. "Thank you for loving me."

* * *

"I'M JUST GOING to freshen up. Give me a few minutes." Whitney said, excusing herself to go to the restroom.

Whitney could feel her phone vibrating from her clutch. It had been vibrating on and off throughout their dinner, but she tried to ignore it. She couldn't ignore it anymore and was grateful Hayden hadn't seemed to have noticed.

Entering the bathroom, she reached into her clutch for her phone. Four missed texts. Three from Ever and one from her mom.

Ever: Everything is set up and ready to go. You're going to go look at the stars and we are going to drive up in a caravan to ambush you guys. Hayden will not suspect anything until it is happening.

Ever: Hayden is going to be so surprised! I can hardly wait! Love you!

Ever: Your mom is insisting on calling you, but I told her you're at dinner. I told her to text you instead. I hope that's okay!

Betty Faris: Whitney dear, sorry I tried calling. Forgot this is all a surprise, for a moment there. I just wanted to tell you that Daddy and I love you. We're so proud of the strong woman you have become. You haven't had an easy time, and we love and support you and Hayden. He is the one you are meant to spend your life with, and we could not be happier. See you soon!

Her phone vibrated with another text. It was her dad. "Dad never texts me," she whispered, opening it.

Dan Faris: I love you, my girl. Hayden is the one.

Whitney felt a tear escape down her cheek, and she quickly sent out three texts:

Whitney to Ever: We're leaving the restaurant now. Will

suggest we go out to the field. I hope this works. If not, I'll drag him there. LOL! Thank you for all your help!

Whitney to Mom: I love you too, Mom! Your support means everything to me!

Whitney to Dad: I love you too, Daddy. Always and forever!

Taking care of her needs quickly and freshening up her makeup, she rejoined Hayden at the table.

"Are you ready?" he asked, rising from the table as she approached.

"Yes, let's go. Are we going to go for a drive?" she asked, trying to keep it casual.

"That's the plan. How about we go to the field again and gaze up at the stars? It's perfectly clear out there tonight."

Yes! she internally cheered. *I didn't even have to bring it up! Everything was going according to her plans.*

"Sounds perfect." She replied, letting him lead her out of the restaurant.

Internally doing a happy dance.

CHAPTER 16

They pulled onto the utility road at Baker's field. The sky was dark, but a faint glow radiated off in the distance.

"What is that?" Whitney asked curiously, squinting at the glow on the road in front of them.

Hayden smiled and continued to drive slowly until they had approached the glow of the lights fully and turned off the truck and headlights. He got out of the truck and came around the front to help Whitney out of the cab. As she rounded the side of the truck, and her eyes widened as she took in what had created the light. On the road was a large heart outline lit by mini metal lanterns. Inside the heart, she could make out the red glow of rose petals.

"What is this?" She asked.

Hayden led her to the middle of the heart. "Wait here," he said. As he went back to the truck and pulled something out of the storage box in the back of the truck.

Approaching her, he was holding a white box tied with a bright red ribbon. He met her gaze and gave her a loving smile. "This is for you," he said, placing the box in her hands. Whitney glanced up at him, her eyebrows raised in question. "Open it," he urged with a smile, gesturing to his gift.

With trembling hands, she pulled the ribbon, letting it fall to the ground. Lifting the lid of the box, her eyes darted up to his, a bright smile curving her lips. "It's my treasure box!" she exclaimed, pulling it out and setting the white box off to the side.

"Open it," he urged again.

Whitney opened it and gasped. Inside was a red velvet box. She glanced up at Hayden, his eyes sparkling in the dim glow of the lanterns.

Hayden took her Treasure Box from her hands and set it gently on the ground. "Whitney Faris, I have a question for you," he said, getting down on one knee and taking the velvet box from her hands. "6 months ago, I professed my love to you right here on this road in the middle of this field under a starry prairie night. That night you told me you felt the same and I can't think of a more perfect place to ask you this question." he paused; his blue eyes gleaming in the moonlight. "Whitney, will you marry me?"

Whitney's eyes filled with tears and her lips curved in a smile that lit up the night. "Yes, I'll marry you, Hayden!"

Hayden got to his feet and swung her around, both laughing and crying with happiness. He set her on her feet and pulled the ring out of the box. "This ring was my mother's, and she told me that someday she would pass it on to me to give to the woman that I wanted to spend the rest of my life with." He told her, sliding the ring onto her finger. "Although I wish she was here, I know she would be so happy to have you wear it."

Whitney glanced down at the beautiful ring on her finger. A simple gold band with a large diamond in the middle and two smaller diamonds on either side, and Whitney had never seen anything more perfect.

"I love it, Hayden." she smiled, wrapping her arms around his neck and crushing her lips to his in a long, delicious kiss. "I can't wait to marry you."

* * *

WHITNEY CAUGHT sight of the vehicle lights turning down the utility road, and a knowing grin curled her lips as Hayden held her in his arms, basking in the glow of their engagement. Hayden's brows furrowed. "I don't know who's coming down here right now, but I'm going to send them away."

Whitney let a giggle escape and Hayden's eyes darted to meet hers, a look of confusion on his face as the vehicles approached. "Hays, it's okay," she reassured, taking both of his hands in hers and giving them a squeeze. "Now, I have a question for you." Whitney countered, transfixing on his gaze. "Will you marry me?" she asked simply.

"Of course, but what is this?" he asked, his eyes widening in surprise as he recognized Ben and Ever's truck, Bea's little Toyota truck and a car he did not recognize pulling in behind them.

The sound of vehicle doors opening and closing and the laughter and calls of their family and friends echoed in the darkness. As they each approached, they all held a lantern like the ones on the road.

Ben, Ever, little Violet and Poppy in their carriers, Bea, Dan, and Betty were all there, as well as Mr. Estes, the local lawyer and marriage commissioner who married Ben and Ever.

Hayden looked at Whitney, a sudden realization washing over his face.

"This is an ambush wedding." she explained. "I want to get married, right now, here in this place that means so much to us both."

Hayden looked into the questioning eyes of their friends and family and back at Whitney.

"Will you marry me tonight?" Whitney asked. "I can't go another day without being your wife."

His eyes flashed with elation at her surprise, and a broad smile overtook his face. Letting out a big, bountiful echoing laugh, he spread his arms wide and lifted his eyes to the starry night sky. "Hell yes!" he shouted into the darkness. "I will marry you right now, here under these stars!"

Everyone cheered and went to work. Bea picked up the boxes from their engagement and putting them into the truck as Dan and Betty embraced Whitney while she showed them her engagement ring. Ben adding several more lanterns to make a makeshift aisle. Mr. Estes taking his position where directed so he could face the couple and Ever handing Whitney a bouquet of red roses. With the scene set, Whitney looped her arm through her father's and beamed up at him. Dan gave his daughter a proud smile, his large hands covering hers. "Let's get you married, sweet girl," he declared gruffly, giving her a nod.

"I'm ready, Daddy."

Bea held up her phone playing "Open Arms" by Journey. The same song they'd danced to at Ben and Ever's wedding.

"I love this song!" both Hayden and Whitney declared aloud.

Everyone laughed as Whitney walked down the candle lit aisle towards Hayden.

"Who gives this woman to this man?" Mr. Estes asked, looking towards her father.

"I do," he answered, clearing his throat.

"I do too." Whitney's mother echoed from behind them, making Whitney roll her eyes.

Dan leaned over and kissed his her on the cheek, placed her hand on Hayden's and walked back to the others.

Hayden took Whitney's hands in his and smiled, his eyes twinkling in the moonlight.

Mr. Estes cleared his throat to begin. "We are gathered here today in Baker's field to witness the marriage of Hayden Hastings to Whitney Faris, under a sea of stars on this glorious prairie night. This couple has wasted no time starting their life together, so we're not going to make them wait another minute longer. Do you have vows?" he asked, looking towards Hayden and then Whitney.

Hayden shrugged and looked at Whitney. "Can we wing it?"

Whitney laughed, causing snickers behind them. "I think we can!"

"Okay then, Hayden you start," motioned Mr. Estes to him.

Hayden's gaze met Whitney's, so soft and tender her heart fluttered wildly. "Whitney, I always searched for my true love, doing strange and often stupid things..." he paused, and he could hear a snicker from Ben and Bea. "To find that one person who was going to fill that void in my heart. That one person who I could share my life with. That would put up with me, would laugh with me and would make me feel whole and happy. Then when I least expected it, on a day that I was there to support my brother finding his happily ever, I met you. There you were, a vision in a green dress. I hadn't even spoken to you yet, and I knew, right then and there, that you were exactly what I wanted." he continued, his voice brimming with emotion. "And as I got to know you more, I found out that you were exactly what I needed. You are my everything, Whitney. The stars, the moon, this entire prairie night sky. Today and for the rest of our lives, I will choose you, Whitney. You are enough and so much more that I deserve. I love you, gorgeous."

Sniffles sounded behind them, and Betty exclaimed. "Oh, good heavens. That was just the sweetest thing I've ever heard."

Everyone laughed through their happy tears, and Mr. Estes gestured to Whitney.

"Hayden, when we met, I thought you were this

impossibly handsome, charming playboy. Someone that was dangerous and would hurt my heart. What you turned out to be was one of the sweetest, kindest, most selfless people I have ever met. And quickly, you became my safe haven. My port in the sea. You are more than I had ever hoped for or thought I would ever have. You have already given me more than I dared to dream, and you have been the sweetest surprise!" she smiled at him; her eyes were wet with tears. "You, Hayden, are my everything. I want to grow old with you, I want to have lots of babies with you, I want to live the rest of my life happily by your side. Every day, I will choose you. I love you, Hays."

"That was beautiful. Rings?" Mr. Estes asked.

Ben stepped forward and handed Mr. Estes two simple gold wedding bands. He handed one to Hayden.

"Do you take Whitney to be your lawfully wedded wife?"

"I DO!" Hayden shouted into the night air.

Whitney took the other band and held it on his ring finger.

"Do you take Hayden to be your lawfully wedded husband?"

"Heck yes, I do!" she exclaimed.

Mr. Estes clasped his hands together and smiled at them brightly. "Then by the power vested in me, by the Province of Manitoba, I now pronounce you officially married! Hayden, you may kiss your bride!"

Hayden took Whitney's face in his hands and looked deep into her eyes. His blue eyes brimming with pure unbridled joy. "My wife," he whispered.

"My husband."

Their lips crashed together, every single emotion, every moment of doubt, everything they had been through worth it, in that life affirming moment. All that was left now was their happily ever after.

EPILOGUE

hristmas, 5 Years later

"BAUER AND BECKETT, it's time to go. Come get your boots and jackets on!" Whitney shouted across the house.

Giggles and the stampede of footsteps echoed down the hallway as two little boys bounded into the front entrance.

"Hey, you two goofballs." Hayden laughed, chasing them, swooping them up into his arms.

Whitney felt her heart flutter at the sight of Hayden with their two oldest sons, Bauer, their eldest now four and Beckett, now three, both spitting images of their daddy with shaggy brown hair and striking blue eyes. A little chubby hand reached out and touched her face gently and she turned to meet the chocolate brown eyes of her third son, one-year-old Bodhi.

She kissed his hand and blonde head softly and smiled

at his sweet cherub face. As she suspected, she and Hayden made the most gorgeous babies.

If anyone would have asked her six years ago, before she met Hayden, if this would be her life, she probably would have laughed at them. Now she was swimming in testosterone, and she loved every minute of it.

Hayden handed her Bodhi's jacket and boots and she set him down on the kitchen island to put them on. After Hayden had suited the other two boys, he rounded the island and leaned over to plant a soft kiss on her lips. His mesmerizing blue eyes grasping hers in their steely gaze. Hayden was still as impossibly handsome as the day she met him and now all these years later she found him even sexier. Seeing him as a doting father was an unexpected aphrodisiac for Whitney, hence her back-to-back pregnancies. He flashed her his devastatingly handsome, panty melting smile and glanced down at their youngest son.

"Do you want to come with Daddy?" he asked Bodhi, putting his arms out to him. Bodhi leapt off the edge, making Whitney's breath hitch in surprise and making Hayden laugh as he caught him. "Don't scare Mommy, you little daredevil."

Whitney shook her head, thankful that all three of her boys were still alive. Raising boys was fun, but scary at times. And they were risk takers, just like their father.

"I'll get the boys into the van and all the presents for the crew are in the back already."

"Thank you, Hays." she breathed out as she reached for the two pies she'd baked on the counter.

Another family Christmas at Prairie Sky.

When they got there, the Farmhouse was alive with

festive excitement. Bauer and Beckett very quickly found their cousins Violet and Poppy and were already upstairs playing in their room, their giggles and voices echoing throughout the house. Ben and Hayden were on baby duty in the living room with Bodhi and Luke. Hayden trying to keep their one-year-old from toppling the tree and Ben trying to make his five-month-old son laugh.

"Luke, I am your father." Ben said in a low, growly voice. The sweet baby boy with brown hair and large hazel eyes breaking into an adorable fit of laughter. Ben and Hayden's deep chuckles wafting into the kitchen.

Whitney sat back in the kitchen chair and smiled at the sweet sounds echoing throughout the house.

"I can't tell you how many times I have heard that line since Luke was born. Pretty sure Ben picked that name because he wanted an excuse to say it." Ever laughed while placing a platter of appetizers on the table. "That's what I get for marrying a Star Wars nerd!"

Whitney laughed and reached for a carrot off a veggie tray. "When are Bea and her crew arriving?" she asked curiously.

"Anytime."

Just then she heard the front door open, and the familiar voice of Bea carried through the front entrance. Bea peeked around the corner, a platter of Christmas cookies in her hands. "Hello Ladies! Merry Christmas! Amelia made these cookies for the kiddos!" Bea exclaimed, setting down the platter and giving Ever a big hug followed by Whitney. "Seriously, procreation station around here! So many kids!"

Ever and Whitney shrugged, laughed, and nodded

their heads in agreement. Whitney smiled at her friends, a gleam in her eye. "Next year we'll have one more." She smoothed over her flat belly and putting her finger over her lips.

"Primrose is about to be taken over by Hastings." Bea whispered. "When did you find out?"

"Last week. Hayden doesn't know yet," she whispered. "It's still early and I'm going to tell him tonight after the boys are in bed."

Ever shook her head and looked from Whitney to Bea. "Do you ever wonder where we would all be if I didn't come back to Primrose?" she asked, raising her wineglass to her lips.

"We would probably be hopelessly single in the city." Whitney added with a smile, looking at Ever.

"And I would likely still be living in my grandmother's house." Bea added, pouring herself a glass of wine.

"Speaking of that, isn't your brother coming home soon?" Ever asked Bea, a look of sadness in her eyes.

"He is." Bea sighed. "He's been officially discharged and will be released. Honestly, I'm just happy Davis is okay."

Whitney reached out and took her hand, giving it a supportive squeeze. A quiet fell on the trio until Bea broke their silence. "Well, let's not bring this party down! Grab your wine or in your case...." she brought her voice to a whisper, gesturing to Whitney. "Sparkling cider. Let's join the men and round up the kiddos in the living room. We got some presents to open!"

* * *

THAT NIGHT they carried in their three exhausted, sugar comatose little boys to their beds. Hayden offered to tuck them in, giving Whitney a welcome reprieve from a busy day. As a working mom, Whitney loved this time of night, when all was quiet and peaceful in the house. She strolled through the house, a flood of memories washing over her as she stopped in front of the Christmas tree, taking in the handmade ornaments and twinkling lights. Additions had been made over the years. The boy's handprints, popsicle stick stars and fun little paper and pipe cleaner crafts from daycare. Whitney smiled hearing the murmur of Hayden tucking the boys into bed and inevitably reading them a quick bedtime story. Next year, their long-planned house renovation would add an upstairs and four extra bedrooms to their modest two-bedroom home, finally giving the boys their own rooms. She couldn't wait. Strolling into the kitchen, she reached into a cupboard, pulling out a glass and filling it at the tap. Taking a long sip of the cold water, she stared out the kitchen window into the darkness of the backyard. The night was clear and the urge to go out into the cold crisp air to see the stars took over. Slipping on her jacket that hung at the back door, she reached for her Jets toque and mittens, the same one Hayden had gifted her on their first date. The set was now faded, the wool pilled, looking a little worse for wear, but she couldn't imagine replacing it. Too many precious memories of hockey games, snowy strolls through evergreen trails and countless nights in the middle of Bakers Field staring up at the stars. Pulling on her boots, she exited through the back door, flicking off the back deck light, immersing her in darkness. Her eyes drifted up to the sky, a universe of stars twinkling down at her, and her hand reached into her pocket. Smiling, her fingers found the gift she had for Hayden hidden inside.

The back door opened, and Whitney glanced over her shoulder to see Hayden, his smile wide and blue eyes shining. Coming up behind her, he followed her gaze, transfixed on the glorious prairie night, a sea of stars above them. "Star gazing?" he asked, wrapping his strong arms around her.

Whitney nodded, and they stood there together, taking in the miraculous view for a long time, wrapped in the warmth of each other's embrace, their noses and cheeks rosy from the cold. Suddenly, a shooting star streaked across the sky, leaving a trail of light against the darkness.

Hayden leaned down, his warm breath and soft lips against her ear. "What did you wish for?" he whispered.

"I can't tell you." she chided with a little giggle.

He nipped her ear playfully, making her squirm in his arms. "Tell me," he insisted, planting sweet kisses along the column of her neck.

"I can't tell you, but I can show you," she replied, turning to face him.

His eyebrows raised in curiosity, she turned to face him. "Put out your hand," she insisted, her eyes dancing in the moonlight.

Hayden obliged, and she reached into her pocket, handing him a wooden star ornament.

"What's this?" he asked, as he squinted to read what it said in the dim light. "Baby's first Christmas. Sorry to tell you, Whit, but this is Bodhi's second..." His eyes widened as realization hit and his eyes darted from the ornament to meet her gaze.

"Are you ready for number four?" she asked, her face glowing with excitement as she added. "And dear lord, please let this one be a girl!" She exclaimed, looking to the heavens.

Hayden laughed and wrapped her in his arms, leaning down to capture her lips in a breathtaking kiss. Pulling back, Hayden looked deep into her eyes, shiny with happy tears. "Thank you, Whitney, for our beautiful family."

Whitney stared up at Hayden, the man she loved more than life itself. A man who healed her heart and gave her a second chance at love. A man who promised her a beautiful life and delivered. Her wish on that shooting star under that glorious prairie night so many years ago, had come true.

* * *

Thank you for reading Prairie Nights.
Want more steamy romance set in the idyllic town of Primrose?
Read Prairie Fire now!

ALSO BY TANYA RENEE

Primrose Series

Prairie Sky

Prairie Nights

Prairie Fire

The Spring of Love Series

By Virginia Taylor

Forever Delighted

Forever Amused

Forever Heartfelt

A New Page

by Aimee MacRae

It Happened in Paris

By Michelle Beesley

Middle Women

By Jack Garrety

Mim and Wiggy's Grand Adventure

By Jay McKenzie

A Dying Second Sun

by Peter A. Dowse

Winner Winner Chicken Dinner

by Sarah Jackson

Resurrection

M H Austin

ABOUT THE AUTHOR

Tanya Renee is a proud Canadian Prairie girl, who grew up on a family farm in Southeastern Manitoba Canada. Always an avid reader, she became intrigued with the romance genre at an early age when she first read Romeo and Juliet. Soon after she started to craft her own stories and poetry and by the time she was in high school, she had declared someday she would become a writer.

Married to the love of her life, she resides in Steinbach, Manitoba, Canada with two teenagers and a menagerie of pets. A kitchen consultant by day and romance writer by night, when she is not cooking up a storm in my kitchen, she can be found tinkering in her garden, drinking copious amounts of coffee with a book in hand, listening to 80's music/audiobooks or at her laptop creating stories that are emotionally satisfying. She writes what she wants to read, epic stories that bring you on a journey and make you believe in love.

www.tanyareneeromance.com

ACKNOWLEDGMENTS

Firstly, I want to thank Sarah Williams, CEO of Serenade Publishing for your wisdom and encouragement and for believing in me.

To the wonderful community of Landmark, Manitoba that inspired my fictional town of Primrose. A place I am so proud to come from and a place I still consider my home.

To my Parents, who taught me that with hard work anything is possible. I hope I make you proud.

To my kids, Theo, and Raina. Dream big, always!

To my husband, Bart, my second and forever love. I am so grateful everyday that the universe brought me to you.

And lastly to all those friends that stood by me when I was going through a very dark time in my life. You know who you are, and I love you.

www.ingramcontent.com/pod-product-compliance
Lightning Source LLC
Chambersburg PA
CBHW020512120726
47904CB00003B/798